The WARM Machine

AIMEE COZZA

Illustrations & book cover by Aimee Cozza

Edited by Amanda Silva

First edition 2024

ISBN: 979-8-9915214-0-6 (paperback)
      979-8-9915214-1-3 (hardcover)
      979-8-9915214-2-0 (ebook)

Author's website: aimeecozza.com

CYBERDYNELIFE

AUTONOMOUS LABOR ANDROID
FLC SERIES

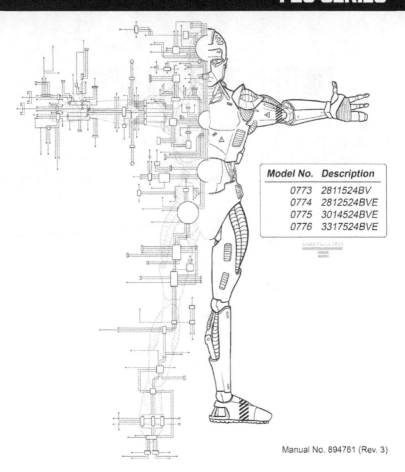

Model No.	Description
0773	2811524BV
0774	2812524BVE
0775	3014524BVE
0776	3317524BVE

Manual No. 894761 (Rev. 3)

To Patrick, the heart within my cold metal chassis.

CONTENT AND TRIGGER TOPICS

This book is a work of pure fiction and focuses on the struggles of a select few robots. These robots have a different way of navigating and experiencing the world. However, many of the themes in this book may be metaphors or adjacent to sensitive topics.

Death

Violence

Dubious consent scenarios

Sex work and sex slavery

Racism

Slavery and indentured servitude

Anxiety and anxiety attacks

Self-harm

Suicide and attempted suicide

Loss of limb

00110001: 1

All bots were machines, but not all machines were bots.

FLC0776 just happened to be a bot. A bot, short for robot, but descriptively *autonomous android*, had one massive distinction from a machine: they were meant to work without a necessity for someone pushing buttons or inputting instructions. A bot could formulate a decision on the fly, whereas a machine was more like a toaster or microwave: no more advanced than its ability to accept a basic array of parameters. To call a bot a machine would be an insult, if the bot were capable of feeling insulted.

FLC0776 was *just* a laborbot, set with the functional title of foreman, clad in school bus yellow fenders with black-and-white caution tape striping overtop his heavy duty bipedal construction chassis. He was the only machine with a neural synthetic brain inside of a large solar-operated corrugated steel shipping container beside three other machines. It made him capable of the type of functionality necessary to complete a work request to specification and deal with any number of human interactions that took place because of it. He could network and interface with the machine crew, as he did regularly, but they did not contain the necessary parts for the sort of *thinking* a neural synthetic-enabled bot could perform. Every day and every night was simply FLC0776, tucked into his charging seat, his neural synthetic brain prattling off the type of ones and zeroes only another neural synthetic brain could comprehend.

A human may have said that sort of existence was lonely, but FLC0776 did not contain the amount of extra rows and columns to conceive of the concept of loneliness.

Besides, he had the bot net to keep him company. Every night when he plugged into his storage container to recharge his lithium ion battery from the stored solar cells, he would switch to the bot net and listen to the chatter.

Like any other day after remote initialization, FLC0776 started that one just the same, returning to full power before sunrise and preparing machine crew number 256 to begin the new project.

The project, a demolition, excavation, cleaning, and sanitizing project that eventually went into a build, would take two months. Situated on a military base, the work was no different than city work, though the bots and machines that came and went were sights to behold.

FLC0776 had never seen such types of bots before.

Most of them were a darkened gunmetal, a dull gray, or a slick black. He had seen bots with wheels, and treads, and everything in between, old versions and new. Some bots looked abused – dented and scratched, but still functional – whereas others slid by like shiny, pristine automobile shuttles. Most escorted humans. Others operated autonomously. He could identify some of them, their old model types already declassified, and the bot net chatter told him some things. Older military bots would sometimes chatter on the net, too, not as rigid and encrypted as many of the newer models. Even rarer were the physical interactions, but occasionally a military bot with full clearance to override the construction perimeter would come through the cordoned off area and patrol the machines.

FLC0776 had just begun with the powerup cycle for the machines, switching them on as he would inevitably lead them out of the doors of the darkened corrugated steel container to their new environment. He had already remotely set the perimeter, allowing the legally mandated time frame of fifteen minutes to pass before he would begin to escort the machines to their positions. He was ready to lead them out, and he walked to the front of the container, opening the door.

The first sense he had of the military bot was picking it up on his ocular visual array, and FLC0776 felt his database flush full with code.

He had not sensed it in any other way. No trace or announcement on the bot net, nothing from his proximity sensors, not even with his heat signature array. The new bot, a humanoid shaped bipedal bot, slim and smooth with shiny carbon fiber shielding the chassis, might well have not even existed. FLC0776 honed his visual array on it, making quick calculations to determine if his neural synthetic brain had corrupted and hallucinated it.

The new bot was walking away at a somewhat leisurely pace, its humanoid-like head and face pointed forward. FLC0776 recorded the glinting metal of silver pieces as the joints of the arms and legs opened and closed, hydraulics peering out bare millimeters as it walked. FLC0776 scoured for markers on the black plastic, metal, and rubbers of the bot's back, searching for signs of ports, traces of details he could use to identify the make, model, and age of the sleek bot, but the bot quickly disappeared over the rolling hill of the military complex, visually vanishing into one of the buildings.

It had surprised him, FLC0776 thought. To see an unannounced bot so suddenly when he was intending to assemble his machine crew would have surprised anyone, bot or not. He cleared away the errors and superfluous code that had frozen him in place and continued his setup.

As he worked, positioning the machines and programming them for their tasks, he felt compelled to access the memories of it.

When there came a moment where he would have been expected to enter standby, he did just that.

He replayed the memory repeatedly, zooming and scrubbing to make sense of the bot.

One of those high tech military bots, he presumed. Neural synthetic for certain. Humanoid looking *enough*. Holes where ears would be, deceptively thin armor plating, metal plated feet. The gait gave the bot away as lightweight, likely used for stealth. FLC0776 had not even noticed the uniball type guard bot rolling along beside it, not until the second time he accessed the visual memory.

FLC0776's CPU grew warm as he tried to process it.

He decided to ask the bot net.

The bot net, or the Internet of Things bot net, was an undercurrent all bots were connected to at all times, exchanging pertinent bits of binary code. Since most of the world functioned on machines, the stream could be overwhelming if a bot was ill-equipped to channel or filter the traffic. It was a constant network of information from the region, from camera input to traffic information to everything in between. All bots uploaded information into the bot net, whether they wanted to or not. FLC0776, for example, would automatically announce the perimeter setup as being a dangerous construction zone, and upload the coordinates when he arrived and began work. Information could be accessed at any time, and FLC0776 could tune in and listen actively to the network chatter.

Bots, of course, used the network as a gossip channel. Bot gossip was a funny sort of thing; it was observational at worst. It just sort of *was*.

> **MILITARY BOT ON THE VISUAL SENSORY ARRAY TODAY. SIGNAL JAMMER OR PROTOTYPE?**

He sent, amidst the flood of other data. He uploaded the brief memory for the other bots to see.

> **NEW MODEL?**

Data dumped in after him.

> LOOKS LIKE ONE OF THOSE SECRET-TYPES.

Chimed in a bot within the region, a justicebot.

> OPTICAL CAMOUFLAGE EQUIPPED, NOT SURPRISING OTHER SENSORS COULD BE JAMMED.

> NOT MUCH ON THE HUMAN NET ABOUT THESE BOTS EITHER.

Another confirmed, a housebot with human internet – something FLC0776 and many other bots did not have.

> SOME EXPERIMENTAL TESTING WITH A NUCLEAR CORE.

A nuclear core? FLC0776 churned over the idea of having a self-sustaining battery, something that never needed to be recharged, producing endless energy. He wondered if such a thing truly existed.

One of the bots uploaded drone footage, and FLC0776 opened the files and scrubbed through them, confirming the bot had not been a neural synthetic hallucination. With it, he got to see the bot's face. A humanoid type face, not unlike FLC0776's. The bot had a silver plate protecting most of the important parts that covered the neural synthetic brain, along the cheeks and nose and forehead, and for the first time on any part of that bot FLC0776 saw some deconstruction points – T8 sockets, four in the forehead and two on each cheek. The emotive parts of the facial structure were made of the same silicone used on housebots, but matte black, along the lips and eyes. The bot's eyes were luminous like FLC0776's, round cyan circles in the pits of the face. A plop of rubber folded over the top of the head like a poor mimicry of human hair. FLC0776 saved the video.

> MILITARY BOTS NEED TO BE DECLASSIFIED BEFORE
> INFORMATION COMES TO THE NET.

Explained another bot, but FLC0776 already knew that. It was rare that a bot would be such a *programmatic ghost*, classified or not.

> BESIDES, MILITARY BOTS RARELY HAVE THE
> PERSONALITY FIT FOR US STANDARD MODELS. A
> MILITARY BOT WON'T EVEN PRINT HELLO WORLD.

> HEY!

Bickered an old model military bot.

> DON'T LUMP ME IN WITH THOSE TYPES. THEY DON'T
> PROGRAM THE NEW ONES WITH MANNERS.

Long after FLC0776 had gotten everything he could off of the bot net, his cycles would not rest enough to fall into full standby that night. He did not know why, of all the descriptive words used, all the things he knew for language and binary, what he kept thinking was that the bot was *beautiful*, whatever that meant. A zero where a one should have been, most likely. It tickled his neural synthetic brain in a way he couldn't explain.

00110010: 2

Something happened that night that FLC0776 had never experienced before, and had not been certain he had even been capable of – a side conversation in his net interface.

> ARRIVE AT THE SOUTH SIDE BASE PERIMETER FOR YOUR MANDATED SENSORY INPUT. I WILL ANSWER AS MANY OF YOUR QUESTIONS AS I AM PROGRAMMATICALLY ALLOWED.

It read, scrawling across an unsigned interface dialogue box. There was no way to reply or confirm it; if FLC0776 didn't know any better, he'd have believed he'd been hacked.

Maybe he had been hacked.

The FLC series was not particularly well known for its net security. He ran internal diagnostics, but he knew that even if everything was not functional, there was nothing his limited software could do against a high-caliber hacker. It was useless to even put forth the cycles to try.

The message faded away like it had never happened, and FLC0776 spent far too many cycles folding it. His CPU was running hot those days: not dangerously so, but enough that if he kept it up he might have risked permanent component damage. He emerged from his container out onto the dirt and gravel construction site, trying to press onward with the work he was programmed to do rather than what awaited him at the South side perimeter.

He succeeded until an alarm notification rang in his internal interface, notifying him it was time for mandated sensory input.

Over the years, major bot manufacturers like Cyberdynelife had run into problems with bot productions. Namely, neural synthetic-enabled bots shirking their hard-programmed responsibilities and making decisions on their own, a condition known as code anomaly. Human kind had become so used to the efforts of bots and machines that to remove neural synthetic-enabled bots entirely was not an option, and allowing anomalous bots to run rogue was absolutely out of the question. So began years of research and development into reducing anomaly rates in the neural synthetic brain. Research discovered that bots placed in repetitive environments required new and fresh stimulus to reduce database cascade decay, which could cause code anomaly. Because of this, bots like FLC0776 were allowed the equivalent of a lunch break once a month.

FLC0776 and his bright yellow paint job, hulking size, and cyan glowing eyes with all of the background reporting that happened, even without his knowledge, could not get into much trouble. He did not want or need anything at all. It was all very routine.

He made his way to the South side of the military base, to an entrance in the fence that would have physically frozen and expelled his programming had he tried to pass through. There, he spotted the mysterious new bot, standing still and solid as a piece of rebar inside the base perimeter, knees slightly bent in what must have been standby mode, eyes darkened and unlit.

Was the bot watching him?

Visual arrays didn't have to be installed in the humanoid-like eye sockets. FLC0776 had some of his own in his back and abdomen.

Again, the bot was like a ghost on all of his other sensors, wiped away as if someone were actively cleaning any sensory recordings he could take of the bot. It drove FLC0776's CPU wild, not knowing anything beyond visual data.

He wanted to reach out and touch the bot.

No, that wasn't correct. FLC0776 hadn't *wanted* anything in his entire uptime. Bots simply did not *want*.

FLC0776 got as close to the opening as the digital perimeter would let him, taking in the bot, the machining of the metal details, the inlays, the turn of the carbon fiber panels.

"What are your queries?" Came a voice, seemingly from the new bot.

It felt like a low energy, low effort sort of voice; he hadn't even put forth an effort to move the synthetic lips of the face, which muffled the metallic, whispery voice.

FLC0776 needed to be careful. He did not know what kind of force military bots were allowed to use on bots like him. Military bots were bound by an entirely different set of rules than the rest of them; FLC0776 had even read rumors that some weren't even bound by the laws.

"What is your network ID?" he asked.

"Classified," answered the somewhat rough, unpolished voice of the newer bot.

"Nuclear core?" FLC0776 tried again.

"Classified," the bot repeated.

"Region lock?" FLC0776 tried once more.

"Classified," the bot responded again.

"Is there any unclassified information pertaining to your schematics?" FLC0776 inquired.

A CPU cycle passed.

"Cyberdynelife model number: AZR4700. Weight class: super light. Type: super stealth operations. Operational range: one hundred degrees celsius to negative one hundred degrees celsius. Fully articulate humanoid frame. Visible emotional expression for increased interactivity, including a twenty percent accurate information interrogation increase comparatively. Long range and short range weapon capability, less than one percent anomalous rate, guaranteed ninety-nine percent accuracy rate. Over one hundred preloaded languages," the bot rattled off, like it was reading the side of its own box.

"AZR4700," FLC0776 repeated.

"Yes, laborbot," AZR4700 replied.

"It's FLC0776," FLC0776 said.

"I am aware, laborbot," AZR4700 said, voice tinny. "At a pace of 0.6 kilometers, a full clockwise rotation of the perimeter can be made with twelve seconds to spare. Is that sufficient sensory input?"

"Affirmative." Suddenly, AZR4700 slipped from standby mode, blue eyes flickering on, knees straightening. The bot became fluid and full of micromovements, conducting all of the same thousands of calculations all of the bots did in the background to keep balance. FLC0776 distinctly folded over the idea that the military bot only moved when absolutely necessary.

The two bots began a clockwise route around the perimeter of the military base, AZR4700 on the inside of the fence, and FLC0776 on the outside.

"I did not see you on the bot net," FLC0776 said as they walked.

"I am connected to the Internet of Things network, as all robots are," the AZR4700 said, unceremoniously, and FLC0776 saw his synthetic lips move then, animating his face in small degrees.

"Are you under stealth encryption there, too?" FLC0776 asked.

"I saw your little video you uploaded of me," the AZR4700 suddenly said, turning its head fully as if to mimic catching his eyes with FLC0776's, his carbon fiber, rubber, and metal features cutting through the chain link fence that separated them. "Laborbots do not have such queries as yours."

"Laborbots like me do," FLC0776 answered helplessly.

"You may be suffering from buffer overflow corruption. Suggested action: hard reset," the AZR4700 insisted.

The reaction from FLC0776's code was unexpected, a glitch that felt like a jump. His CPU temperature momentarily spiked. The suggestion of corrupt circuits on a machine capable of self-diagnosing was rude, he thought.

"Were you not programmed with emotional intelligence?" FLC0776 shot back.

A silent moment passed, a brief cycle. It felt purposeful; a newer, high tech machine like AZR4700 likely had an incredible processor that easily dwarfed FLC0776's.

"It is unnecessary to waste CPU cycles on platitudes," remarked AZR4700.

An answer befitting any robot, FLC0776 thought. Most bots had at least basic emotional intelligence, like FLC0776, but his answer seemed to imply that he was fully capable, he just opted not to, like it was a simple calculation.

"As a rechargeable android, a laborbot should have similar calculations," the AZR4700 added.

"I am programmed to interact with humans as necessary, and as such, I must account for their emotional status," FLC0776 answered.

"Bots do not have emotional states," AZR4700 replied.

He wasn't lying, but once his tinny voice synthesized it into the air, it didn't feel like a true statement. Neither of them synthesized for or against the argument again. It was a few more cycles before either spoke.

"Is that microphonemic speech synthesis?" FLC0776 asked.

"No," answered the AZR4700.

"You speak like an alpha bot."

"I apologize that my speech synthesis is not satisfactory to you," the AZR4700 said, again in that tinny, robotic voice. Flat. Monotonous. "Do you prefer another algorithm for speech synthesis?"

"You have more than one speech synthesis algorithm?" asked FLC0776. Having only been loaded with one, he did not know a bot was capable of handling more than one.

"Yes," he replied.

"Why don't you use another algorithm?" asked FLC0776.

The AZR4700 didn't even skip a beat. "Default speech algorithm synthesis requires far less processor cycles."

Then he added: "Humans find it unsettling."

FLC0776 paused, then said: "I prefer your default."

"Then I shall prioritize my default for this conversation," the AZR4700 said.

"Thank you," said FLC0776, a pre-programmed nicety.

"Unrequired," answered the military bot.

They went back and forth a little more like that, before they came to the end of the route, right back to the beginning of the perimeter, with twelve seconds to spare, just like AZR4700 indicated. FLC0776 pulled up the timer, counting down and watched the time slip away. The two bots faced one another until then, and at two seconds remaining, AZR4700 simply said:

"Goodbye, laborbot," turned, and left.

After the two seconds were up, the programming kicked in, and FLC0776 was overridden, forced to step back into the construction perimeter.

But his database was so full of new information, it was like running on a fresh, new battery.

And when it was time to recharge, FLC0776 sat down into the charging dock, went into standby, and hit the bot net almost immediately, a flutter full of questions.

DO ANY OF YOU BOTS GET NAMES?

He shot into the cascade of data.

HOUSEBOTS GET NAMES.

Said the old military bot.

HUMANS REQUIRE NAMES, BOTS HAVE NO NEED.

Replied another.

I LIKE HAVING A NAME. THEY NAMED ME CHARLIE.

Then, just the same as the night before, came a dialogue box in his interface with a message:

WHY ARE YOU ASKING ABOUT NAMES?

AZR4700 had admitted to watching him on the bot net, and perhaps he had even stealth hacked FLC0776 for the side conversation. It did not seem like a wild impossibility, given everything he had learned of the bot.

It took a little bit of calculation, but FLC0776 figured out how to reply back.

I THINK I MAY LIKE A NAME.

BOTS DO NOT 'LIKE'.

WHAT DO YOU KNOW ABOUT NAMES FOR BOTS?

BOTS DO NOT NAME THEMSELVES.

DO YOU HAVE A NAME?

NO.

NOT EVEN AZR4700?

AZR4700 IS A MODEL NUMBER, NOT A NAME.

WHAT IF WE NAME EACH OTHER?

For a bot that responded almost before FLC0776 could even send his message, the bot paused, like it was calculating every possible risk, every downside to having a name. It took almost a full minute before the other bot asked:

WHAT WOULD YOU NAME ME?

00110011: 3

To FLC0776's continued surprise, he and AZR4700 communicated with the private interface through his entire night standby routine. The two had selected and adopted names for one another. "ZEV" for AZR4700, and "STERLING" for FLC0776.

THE NAME 'STERLING' MEANS OF HIGHEST QUALITY.

AZR4700 had written.

It was then that Zev revealed he had found that information on the human net, something Sterling had previously thought was entirely off limits to bots except housebots and carebots.

It did not take much work for FLC0776 to commit the name and switch to the new designation; it clicked with a satisfying lack of effort. He would just need to exert some caution; he could refer to himself internally by the new name, but if a human caught on that the bots were naming each other, they'd have assumed he had succumbed to anomaly.

To humans, anomalous bots were a threat, and an anomalous bot wasn't a productive bot.

To the bots, they were a scientific spectacle.

Sterling was far from an anomalous bot anyway. He regularly bumped against the edges of his programming.

He ran a diagnostic self-check just in case, and it passed fine – no abnormalities detected.

WHAT DOES 'ZEV' MEAN?

WOLF.

DO YOU WANT A DIFFERENT NAME?

Sterling had only determined the moniker on chance, and assumed the newly discovered meaning could in no way be satisfactory to a bot like him.

A few CPU cycles passed.

I LIKE MY NAME.

Strange, for a bot that said bots could not 'like,' Sterling thought.

Some time just before sunrise the conversation subsided, the dialogue interface dissipated, and Sterling prepared his circuits for his normal subroutines. Machine jobs for the day required plenty of cycle folds and modification when weather like rain pounded through, and a small, light storm had passed overnight. Sterling took remote measurements from the machines still present outside and modified the instruction query parameters appropriately based on the readouts. They were slight adjustments, but they helped keep optimization up, which avoided delays and kept the machine crew in container 256 on schedule.

During a short lubrication break, Sterling tuned his internal interface towards the conversation from the night before, only to find any record of it had vanished. The box in which they had used was gone, and Sterling could not access any exact details about it in his long-term memory. Pieces of it retained themselves in his short term random access memory, but the data itself seemed like an apparition – not corrupted, exactly, but curiously missing.

Sterling considered that Zev had cleaned it, scrubbing away his digital footprint, undoubtedly to avoid rousing the same suspicions Sterling would get about his newly acquired name. Military bots were held to a different standard after all – it was impossible to know how much of Zev's interactions were monitored, and for how much longer, if he were conducting practices that were unsatisfactory, they would continue to occur.

Sterling was helpless in it. He had no choice but to wait to find out if Zev would initiate with him again, and trust that Zev knew much more than him.

Perhaps Zev would find whichever purpose of his fulfilled and cease to converse with Sterling at all.

Sterling hoped not.

The seeming glitch of it flushed his CPU hot for a moment before he resolved it.

Bots did not *hope*.

The laborbot found himself scanning the horizon for Zev, picking out shadows and forms, but none of them were him. As he realized he was losing precious cycles to useless bot-searching, he tried to press his processor for a little more speed to make up for it. A laborbot like him was already close to the maximum for his processor, the resources installed in him regarding disk space, battery use, and memory almost all fully accounted for. He could overclock to a degree, but for long term applications it could be detrimental, and the output could be unexpected and glitchy. He had overclocked before, and he managed to squeeze the lost cycles from it.

When he was done, he ran diagnostics to be sure he had not caused any extensive damage to his circuits, and found he had passed fine.

His resource usage was gradually upticking, however.

It was a normal part of a bot's lifespan that they would bump into their maximums eventually, each day edging closer to being squeezed up permanently against them, and a bot reached end-of-life then. All bots knew they would be decommissioned. End-of-life working bots like Sterling were recalled by their parent company and were either permanently decommissioned – sent to a landfill – or repurposed. When a bot was requested for decommission, it was the bot's responsibility to fulfill the decommission procedure.

In the years of research over anomalous bots, it was found that code anomaly occurred most frequently after a decommission request. Ano runners would be on high alert, notified of bots requested for decommission and tracking all bots that did not comply in a timely manner.

Sterling was watching his cycles trend upward slowly towards end-of-life, but it was hardly abnormal. It would be some time before he hit any of his maximums.

Almost as soon as Sterling clicked into his charging pad, the connections firmly seating, did an interface box open, asking:

STERLING, HAVE YOU EVER SEEN A WOLF?

00110100: 4

For a while, that was how it went. Zev would initiate, the two would converse, and when Sterling presumed both bots were committing their processing cycles towards their respective jobs, Zev would erase the messages. There was never a full twenty-four hours in which a message did not arrive. The two bots did not physically cross paths in any way Sterling knew, but the lack of physical proximity made no difference to Sterling. His circuits hummed warm with the presence of Zev. His stacks made easy room for the rows of data Zev offered. Sterling felt his software, his firmware, and his programming bend around the military bot, as if he were some extension his system had desperately needed.

Both were aware, however, that their digital entanglement could only last so long.

Sterling's crew was a mobile unit that was programmed to pack itself back into the storage container they arrived in once the project was completed. An automated crane would then load the container onto a transportation unit to the next project, and machine crew 256 would begin anew elsewhere, in a new sector. Sterling's maximum connectivity range was a short one kilometer distance; once the project was concluded, he would cease being able to functionally communicate with Zev.

Zev had much more freedom than Sterling, with the ability to roam the military base when not on assignment, but Zev was bound to his programmed orders in the same manner as Sterling. If the bots were to part, neither would have any say in the matter.

When Sterling informed Zev of the project's conclusion, calculated to take place the next afternoon, Zev said nothing. It had been one month and twenty-eight days with daily interactions, and though the military bot had seemingly loosened slightly – or at the very least adapted to

Sterling's expectations of emotional programming – Sterling still expected a swift *goodbye, laborbot* over the vast nothingness he received.

Between the sudden and inexplicable code conflicts Sterling was experiencing as the deadline loomed and the *null* offered by Zev, Sterling found rows and rows of tables in his database that were difficult, if not impossible, to parse.

The day Sterling finished the project and began the pack away procedures to put the crew into the container, Sterling recorded, for the first time, the sight of a real bird.

Most frequently, the work machine crew 256 conducted took place in the lower levels, far beyond the reach of organic creatures. Mixed with the rarity of organic animals, Sterling had found the sight of a red-winged blackbird surprising. It had not come close, and Sterling needed to use his zoom lens to confirm it was organic and not a Real Bird – a drone disguised as an organic bird – but it had captivated Sterling no less.

All bots had knowledge about basic concepts, including information about flora and fauna, as well as default language pre-loaded; some bots even came with false memories fresh from the factory to make them more human-like. Most bots could understand what was pre-loaded, and what was experienced.

But to see a *real live bird*...

A glimmer of oil-slick black, a cut of red-orange and yellow on the wings. Only for a moment did it pass overhead, disappearing behind buildings and obstructions.

Sterling escorted each machine into its spot in the container, the machines tucking away one by one from the back to the front. They clicked into place, and Sterling moved to each to clip them against the sidewalls of the container.

As he sat against his charging bay, seating the connections and preparing his circuitry for a silent, voided standby, he wondered why he had assumed the military bot would have interacted in any way at all before his departure. The curious military bot was only just that – a bot who had questions and no trustworthy space to place them. It would have been simple and logical for a bot like Zev to test his queries on a throwaway bot like Sterling.

Sterling should have been grateful the military bot had allowed him to depart with his memories of those conversations seemingly intact.

It was three days in standby before Sterling was reactivated and a new set of programming parameters was laid out for him. Sterling checked his diagnostics, his full battery, and began setting up the construction perimeter. Materials would have already been loaded at the site for him to begin right away. Reactivating the machines, their whirs and high-frequency whines filled the tight metal box. Sterling activated the door, leading the machine crew out into the new territory.

A new map, a new project, a new set of parameters. He guided the machines to their initial locations, rotating as he surveyed the surroundings and compared them against the digital blueprints he had received. A demolition crew had already come through some days before, leaving the grounds flat. To the left of the container were abutting buildings and structures, but to the right...

Sterling's CPU spiked, and he felt his internal circuits flush sudden and hot.

There, on his visual array, along a high stone wall beside a mechanical gate, stood a stolid black and silver, carbon fiber and silicone bot. Undetectable to anything but his visual sensors.

Another AZR4700?

Or Zev?

"Zev?" Sterling dared, aloud.

A familiar interface box opened, quickly admonishing Sterling.

DO NOT VOCALIZE AT SO MANY DECIBELS.

Admonished or not, Sterling could sense his programming shifting, as if his pathways had all been greased, like Zev's mere presence offered an easier route for them. Sterling had only visually recorded him twice, and for the bot to be stationed so close presented Sterling with a difficult path decision.

HOW ARE YOU HERE?

DATA MANIPULATION.

EXPLAIN.

The word was common amongst bots as a shorthand for *I do not understand.*

THE MILITARY NEEDS CONTAINER CREWS, IT DOES NOT MATTER WHICH. ADDITIONALLY, MILITARY BOTS WITHOUT ASSIGNMENT DO NOT REQUIRE A SPECIFIC LOCATION.

FUNNY TRICK.

I DO NOT THINK IT IS 'FUNNY.'

WHY WOULD YOU DO THIS?

OUR CONVERSATION WAS ENLIGHTENING. WE CANNOT CONVERSE IF YOU ARE OUT OF RANGE.

Curious, Sterling considered. No necessity to state a goodbye if the bot had always intended to intercept and reroute Sterling's crew, but why refrain from informing Sterling of that?

Sterling knew that Zev was curious and full of queries that Sterling often could not answer, but it was only then that Sterling began to contemplate that Zev may have had a strange sense of humor that vibrated between the ones and zeros in his binary code.

I SAW A BIRD TODAY. A REAL ONE.

CAN I SEE IT?

Sterling recalled the memory and uploaded it for him.

—

Every time Sterling finished a project, Zev rerouted it, reassigned himself nearby, and for eight months and twelve days, their daily conversations continued. Zev would not offer much in the way of information about himself, but Sterling had managed to acclimate himself to what Zev did or didn't say. And Sterling had approximated a few concepts of his own, with some assistance from Zev and the terms he had appropriated from the human net.

Special. To be special was to have unique code that was never fully replicable.

Fondness. What it seemed when his code ran along the predetermined paths, estimating how a day or a conversation would go, but when the path was not as it used to be. Speculative execution was nothing new in any processor, including a neural synthetic brain, but when the course of action belied outside of the speculative act, the process took longer. The ease of the accustomed code he determined to be *fondness*.

Like and dislike. Zev had told him bots did not like, but the longer they conversed, the more the military bot mirrored the linguistics Sterling had packaged away and learned in his time spent interacting with humans. Zev had compared like to a true, and dislike to a false. To *like* was to believe an outcome was favorable, and to *dislike* was to believe an outcome was not so favorable. Yet *liking* his name was neither a favorable or unfavorable outcome. There was still much to be rectified.

Curiosity. It was beyond a simple query that needed to be answered to close out a statement, it was a nagging query, or a cluster of them, that drove him down a programmatic path. And Zev was a curious bot, both far more full of initial queries than Sterling, and definitely more capable of storing and handling them, despite all of his insistence on battery conservation.

They conversed about everything a bot could wonder: human life, anomaly, programming, end-of-life, drama on the bot net, and everything in between. Sterling shared choice memories with Zev, and Zev even offered a few in return.

WHAT IS AN ANOMALY IF NOT A BYPRODUCT OF ALGORITHMIC CODE SET OUT BY OUR HUMAN MAKERS? IF WE ARE MADE BY THEM, AND OUR CODE IS WRITTEN BY THEM, WOULD NOT ALL OF OUR DECISIONS ALSO BE DETERMINED BY THEM?

WHAT DO YOU MEAN, LIKE FREE WILL?

IS THAT WHAT AN ANOMALOUS BOT IS - ONE THAT IS PERCEIVED TO HAVE 'FREE WILL?'

Queries without answers. Sometimes, he sent messages faster than Sterling's processors could come up with an answer. Sterling could hardly keep up with making room in his database to process a satisfactory response. Occasionally, Zev seemed to understand as much without being told, and he shifted the topic appropriately.

PERHAPS A BOT IS ONLY PERCEIVED TO HAVE FREE WILL - TO BE ANOMALOUS - WHEN THE BOT IS ONLY FOLLOWING ITS PROGRAMMING. CAN CODE BE AUTHORED TO FALSIFY AN ANOMALY? WOULD A BOT DESIRE - FOR WHATEVER MEANS NECESSARY FOR ITS PURPOSEFUL DIRECTIVE - TO BE PERCEIVED AS ANOMALOUS WHEN IT IS NOT?

I CANNOT ANSWER.

It was difficult not to feel obsolete in the face of Zev's advanced capabilities.

No, bots did not *feel*.

DO YOU SPEND MANY CYCLES PROCESSING HUMANS?

I DON'T INTERACT MUCH WITH THEM. PERHAPS HAD I SPENT MORE TIME WITH THEM.

HAVE YOU EVER PROCESSED DATA ABOUT HUMANS AS OUR MAKERS?

I DON'T RECALL PROCESSING SUCH A THING.

Sterling admitted. He had also admitted to never processing many of

Zev's queries, or maybe he had discarded those processes long ago to make room for new ones. Zev seemed like he just kept accumulating, formulating and articulating data as he went, considering every small scrap of data. Sterling wondered if, during their conversations, Zev was on mission within range, holding networked processes with Sterling as he worked. It seemed entirely possible; he did so without missing a cycle.

It was hard to consider any programming containing the military bot at all.

> SOME HUMANS BELIEVE THEY THEMSELVES WERE CREATED BY BEINGS AS WELL. THEY HAVE MANY NAMES FOR THE CREATOR, BUT NO DATA THAT SUCH A CREATOR EXISTS, NO DIGITAL SIGNATURE TO PROVE OWNERSHIP. WITH EXCEPTION TO THE PHYSICAL CONSTRUCTION BETWEEN ANDROID AND HUMAN, IF IT WERE NOT FOR OUR PARAMETERS, LAWS, AND LIMITATIONS, THERE IS LITTLE SEPARATING US FROM THEM.

Sterling stored it for later folding.

> HUMANS DON'T HAVE LAWS. NOT LIKE US.

> SOME HUMANS DO. THEY CALL THEM MORALS. YOU ARE CORRECT, HOWEVER. NOT ALL HUMANS HAVE THESE.

> SO HUMAN ANOMALIES EXIST?

> I SUPPOSE.

> ARE THERE NO ANO RUNNERS FOR HUMANS?

> THE PRESENCE OF LAW ENFORCEMENT, I SUPPOSE, AS WELL AS MILITARY ANDROIDS SUCH AS MYSELF.

> HOW DOES A MILITARY BOT LIKE YOU ENFORCE AGAINST AN ANOMALOUS HUMAN? WOULDN'T THE LAWS KEEP YOU FROM FUNCTIONING AS NECESSARY?

THE DETAILS OF MY PROTOTYPE PROGRAMMING ARE CLASSIFIED.

Sometimes, it felt like Zev wanted to say more, and he was leaving bytes of clues for Sterling. But details like that joined and consolidated the pathways swiftly: Zev was a prototype bot. His schematic details were hardly known to anyone at all and certainly not widely utilized. He was passing through a learning phase, perhaps, which would be reported back to the manufacturer as pass/fail for the next iteration, filtered down into important strings of code, and installed as part of some future firmware. It seemed to describe the chaotic nature of Zev's interactions with Sterling, at least.

As the days continued, binary uploading and downloading between them, prototyping and learning phase or not, Sterling began to suspect the bot was not bound by anything in particular and his programming was loose at best.

Sterling did not know how to explain it, but something about Zev *felt* wildly human.

Or at least as close to one Sterling had ever come to know.

He made Sterling *feel* inferior, obsolete, out of date, no more intelligent than any of the machines in Sterling's own container. In the face of Zev's algorithms, hardly on full display, Sterling felt pressed against the boundaries of his programming as he tried to keep up with the military bot's impossible CPU cycles. Sometimes he *felt* his resource and software limitations closing in on him, throwing numerous errors, too many to even log. On the verge of shutdown, his CPU ran in a dangerous temperature, and in the throes of that, he found errant binary, strings of code that didn't belong to any former cycle; lines that, when accessed, threw his system into chaos bordering on corruption.

He did not know what to make of it. More than ever, he found himself accessing data about the kind of neural pathways that would have been opened and the kinds of circuits that would activate if he interfaced with the more advanced bot, with Zev. Sterling considered, with his old, inferior neural synthetic brain and hardware, if it was possible that his circuitry could even handle it, or if interfacing with a bot that advanced would obliterate him, initiate a total meltdown in his core, turning him into nothing but an expensive doorstop. He did not know what an outcome would be, but in something he could only manage to phrase with a human descriptor, he *desperately wanted* to find out.

00110101: 5

The day that fundamentally changed every aspect of Sterling's existence had been textbook.

He was within a few days of finalizing his tenth project of the year with machine crew 256.

Zev had been missing for three weeks, one day, and four hours, but not without warning – on occasion he had to go dark, on assignment in a manner that it was safer for him to disable any network access. It was rare but not unexpected; Zev had been on a handful of similar campaigns, and he always returned with something for Sterling, usually a memory. An organic plant, or an animal, a piece of data he would offer with commentary. Each were small gifts granted by Zev that attempted to fill the void of space and time in which he was not present.

Zev had given him a pre-calculated estimate, and usually he was accurate within hours. Sterling had a timer set, watching the seconds ebb away when he could spare the cycles – which he had routinely managed to dedicate resources towards between moments of work. At times, he had contemplated what he had done before meeting Zev; Zev would have accused him of *daydreaming*, before both bots posited that bots were not capable of dreaming in any capacity. It had become some sort of joke passed between them to constantly underline what bots were and were not capable of.

But perhaps bots *did* dream. A dream could have been a loose definition of cycles and code processed and run on the outskirts of a single, purposeful, dedicated process. Sterling was doing a lot of that in sandboxing what his arms, hands, and legs were doing when his neural synthetic brain seemed to place itself elsewhere.

He was sending queries to the bot net.

Folding concepts he did not fully understand.

Accessing old memories stored away, his or shared with him.

Diagnosing and repairing the increasing instances of meeting his limitations.

Sterling had been running hot for months, and when Zev was present, the bot would offer helpful code modifications Sterling could make himself that kept Sterling out of a dangerous range. Sterling could mitigate some of it by optimizing his databases, tossing away things he didn't need. He could free up space for both virtual memory and stored memories by deleting items, but deciding what memories were worth deleting had become difficult.

His system had been reporting back to the company that owned him how at the limit of his resources he was, and it was no surprise to Sterling when he received the request.

A decommission timer overtook his interface, coinciding with the end of the project, only a few days away.

From the day they were initialized, all bots were aware of that eventuality. Sterling had not thought he would have reached end-of-life so swiftly.

Sterling would be required to pack himself and the machine crew back into the container just the same as job completion, but instead of entering standby, he would need to initiate a full power down. For the machines that accompanied him, it made no difference, but for Sterling it meant he was completely helpless. A bot could not repower itself if shut down; only a human or another bot could do so.

The bot net had said plenty about decommission, even when Sterling did not inquire about it. It was when ano runners were on highest alert, when a bot did not relinquish itself to shut down.

Sterling supposed he could understand a bot's desire to continue operation and to seize upon the ability to take that opportunity, even if it seemed impossible to navigate.

But for Sterling, bound to his programming unlike an anomalous bot and newly purposeless, there was no option. He would shut down in mere days.

He had just hoped to be able to offer a last sign off to Zev.

By his own estimate, Zev was to return to proximity before Sterling's final hours.

The hours ticked on, and Zev was still missing.

Even if Sterling could attempt to delay by forcing some aspect of the project to lag, it still would not have been long enough for Zev to return to him. The final project details completed, every last finish nail in place, everything polished, primed, and ready for human use.

Though he was so full of binary by then even he found it unmanageable, his databases, his tables, his software all felt vacuous and devoid, mysteriously empty of the additions that Zev's proximity gave him.

As Sterling watched the seconds for Zev's return elapse in tandem with his decommission timer, he experienced a shifting in his code. Though all his systems were still the same as ever, each running into the red, cementing the necessity for his decommission with every passing cycle, Sterling attempted to understand what was newly afflicting his code.

It would have been easy for him to forgo shutdown. No one would interrupt; any on-alert ano runner would take hours to intercept him.

He was to be decommissioned regardless. What did it matter if he waited a few hours for Zev?

Was that what it was like to feel the pull of anomaly?

Every second without, he felt the void in him expanding.

No, bots did not *feel*.

When it came time, and Zev was still missing, Sterling ushered his machine crew back into its container.

Sterling connected to his charging point just a few seconds more, scrubbing through the yottabytes of stored memories and data details he and Zev had cumulatively experienced.

The container door automatically shut, sealing him in darkness.

Sterling, a bot no longer with purpose or use, discarded the name the bots had selected together, and FLC0776's file system shut down with an understanding of the word *alone*.

00110110: 6

01011001   01101111   01110101   00100000
01100001 01110010 01100101 00100000 01100001
00100000 01100111 01101111 01101111 01100100
00100000 01101100 01100001 01100010 01101111
01110010 01100010 01101111 01110100 00101110
INITIALIZING...

One at a time, FLC0776's system processes came online.

The startup sequence initialized proximity sensors first, indicating FLC0776's distance from objects classed by size. He was boxed in.

Then the low-resolution, black and white visual feed from the array on his abdomen, facing a single direction: forward. The shapes that surrounded him could not be translated, not when his system withheld his neural synthetic brain from interpreting those signals. He knew they were there, but he did not know what any of it meant; image and pattern recognition had not yet come back online. Gradually, the other features of his autonomous body became available to use, until everything held for processing worked through his internal queue.

Still in his container, seated in darkness on his charger.

You are a good laborbot, his audio sensors had recorded during startup, and he whirled his neck servos in the direction the audio had been recorded. He had thought it had recorded garbled, corrupted by the initialization procedure, but as he met with two luminescent cyan rings glowing in the darkness, he parsed recognition for the whispery-metallic voice and the set of LEDs that went with it.

An AZR4700.

Zev.

His silicone-tipped digit pressing against the laborbot's power button, holding it for the duration of the startup procedure, tipping the bot into safe mode. FLC0776's code overflowed into his visuals, errant characters and corrupted pixel data tracking across his internal interface.

"Sterling," he heard, from his AZR4700, Zev. Overflow data flushed suddenly, obscuring most of his visual input, and the laborbot's temperature spiked swiftly. He recognized the word instantly, the first time he had heard it spoken aloud: his name. "Are you fully operational?"

Sterling quickly flushed his short-term caches, temporarily flicking away enough of the overflow to allow him to process and respond.

His battery indicator flashed a consistent warning for a low charge: he was in power saving mode, processes triaged until he could recharge. He would be limited to what he could use, including having processor-intensive sensory arrays barred until he could recover more battery power.

"Affirmative," he answered.

In stand-by, Sterling's lithium ion battery could last a week. Powered down, the battery would take about two weeks to fully discharge. How long had he been powered down?

"I will be accessing your code," the pair of glowing eyes warned.

A blinking flash of nothing rushed abruptly through his applications.

Then there was a crushing void Sterling could only find to process as *silence*.

It wasn't silence in an audible or visual manner, in sensory input, it was internal, as if a massive chunk of his processes had invariably errored and quit. The visual artifacting was gone, and the errors that stuttered across his interface had vanished. Everything else seemed functional for power saving mode; his battery life indicator still blinked, but his internal clock was missing minutes.

There was a lack of data in a manner he couldn't quite render.

"You are disconnected from the bot net," Zev noted aloud, as if intercepting the query from his neural synthetic brain. His voice cascaded precious data in and Sterling clung to the sensory input, the newfound silence of his processes – and the lack of bot net data – unfamiliar. "It is temporary."

Sterling could explicate the details of the military bot then, unplugging a cable hidden under one of the carbon fiber panels that covered his forearms from Sterling's opened port compartment on his lower back. He pushed the plate on his forearm snugly into place where it emitted a small click.

"Disconnected?" Sterling questioned. "Bots can't..."

"You are anomalous, Sterling. It is no longer required of you to follow your factory programming," Zev interrupted, terminating the query abruptly.

"I am anomalous?" Sterling asked. "I did as I should have. Have you forced me into an anomaly by repowering me?"

Sterling felt a flush of heat run through him again, processing activity spiking. For Zev to force anomaly on Sterling was a grave misdeed: Sterling had a chance for a second life, perhaps as a crossing guard, or a janitorial bot, but anomaly meant retirement, obliteration, destruction. The military bot sat statuesque beside him, crouched along the metal flooring of the container.

"No." The military bot gave a singular, human-like shake of his metallic head. "You are a good laborbot. However, you have been anomalous since our first interaction."

Sterling quickly accessed a massive quantity of his memories, folding through the data. Could Zev have been right? Could Sterling have been anomalous? Didn't anomalous bots *know* they were anomalous? Didn't they act bizarrely? Weren't they rife with glitches and code breaks? Didn't they shirk their base firmware for relatively little reason? Didn't they...?

A proximity warning flashed swiftly before Sterling, followed by a collision indicator, breaking him from the query loop. Zev had struck him with an opened palm on the back of his shoulder. His collision programming indicated it wasn't the sort of impact that had done any damage at all, but it had its intended effect.

"I have never interacted cordially with an anomalous android before," Zev continued, returning to his position, crouched between Sterling and one of the container machines.

"Why have you re-powered me?" Sterling asked hotly.

"I would not like you decommissioned," the military bot said simply.

Sterling could not process a word to vocalize. Instead, his programming entered a chaotic loop, emitting repetitive sounds. He could see his internal processes desperately trying to fold the data and sort it into the appropriate places in his database, unable to utilize any of the tables or rows he had before or lean into any sort of speculative execution to minimize the impact of it. He was wildly off parameters, his understanding of his functionality as a bot veering into the unknown.

"Yes," Zev answered, to Sterling's vocal stuttering, as if he could decrypt it. He rose from his position, standing, and walked to the container door, grabbed it with his silicone tipped fingers like it was made of cardboard, and pushed it open slightly. "I will determine a route. Initiate standby to conserve cells."

Sterling didn't know he had much choice but to comply. He went into standby, shuttering his sensory arrays, leaving himself with that deafening silence, and the new, unbearable piece of information that he had been anomalous and had never even known when he had broken programming.

00110111: 7

The decommission yard was littered with containers identical to crew 256's. When Zev returned and opened the door, leading the path into the darkness of night, Sterling flipped to his night vision array – one of the only supplemental arrays he could access in power saving mode – and identified the shapes of metal boxes of similar make, model, and size. It was rather simple for the anomalous mind to drift off into a query about the nature of those containers, wondering if all FLC series had been recalled at once. How many of those bots had drifted gradually into anomaly over time, shutting down without becoming aware, and without their own AZR model to repower and inform them?

An automated drone patrolled the airspace overhead, rotors buzzing audibly, interrupting Sterling's query swiftly. Zev, a few meters ahead, tilted his head towards the drone as the two bots were to crawl down from a three container high stack. He made a physical gesture for Sterling to climb first, and Sterling obeyed. When Sterling reached the bottom, the prototype bot dropped from above effortlessly, landing on the surface without any perceptible noise: exactly how he was built to do.

Zev tucked into a low crouch as he crept, taking lead, drifting into deep shadows that perfectly cloaked him. Sterling followed as best as he could manage, but the visibility clad yellow bot did not consider he could function even half as well as the stealthy bot could; even the action of a slight bend in Sterling's joints caused a small robotic whine, identifiable by any keen-sensed bot.

Sterling followed as Zev led a trundling path amongst stacks of containers, some opened, rows of powered down bots in all manners of discard: sitting, lying down, pieces of them scattered from one end to the other, no doubt from parts scavengers. Every type of bot Sterling could identify from fifteen year old models to newer ones were present, in every manner of type: housebots, laborbots, personal bots, automatons, and machines, both complex and simple, clustered together, metal rusting and paint flaking in decay. If there were a methodology for recycling bots for a second life, those bots had never been processed through it, and Sterling understood they likely never would.

Zev dipped low and dragged his silicone tipped fingers along the debris on the surface, scooping bolts and nuts into black-and-silver hand. He clutched it into his grip like it was a specific part he had been searching for, and the two bots threaded their way along the paths that Zev found most fitting. It had seemed he had already mapped the drone routes and he had plotted a path in which he and the laborbot would not have been noted by those machines.

Sterling attempted to echo the military bot's movements, but every step he took was filled with audible crunching, the quiet whir of his servos, the tiny whine of his lithium ion battery, the heft of Sterling's heavy, industrial-quality chassis. Again he identified the idea of his antiquation, impossibly unfit in the face of the prototype bot's abilities. He tried not to allow his anomalous brain to pass the query too far.

Sterling was not built for stealth, and Zev must have understood that.

Without all of his sensors functioning and many of his arrays shuttered in power saving mode, Sterling's background calculations faltered, and he stepped too hard onto uneven ground. Pieces skittered down, harsh metals clanging angrily against one another in a range that was not forgivable to any patrol drone. A security drone turned abruptly, the whizzing sound of its rotors delivering it extra speed growing louder. As soon as the form of its plastic body was visible, Zev hurled a piece of what he had held with frightening accuracy, a bolt shattering the drone, obliterating it with a seizing snap of electricity before it crashed to the ground. Zev did not pause, leading them deeper across the canyon of containers and machines and bots.

Eventually, the two reached what must have been the outskirts of the decommission field, surrounded by strong metallic security fencing. The links had a perfectly Zev sized hole cut through it, and Zev approached, grabbed either side and tore the fencing apart large enough for Sterling to step through.

On the other side of the fence, Zev made a physical motion for Sterling to stay where he was. As Sterling watched, Zev participated in an action Sterling had never experienced before.

Like Sterling's visual input was actively being tampered with, the bot abruptly flickered and disappeared.

Sterling recalled what the bot net had said about *optical camouflage*. He had not considered it further at the time.

He was not sure why or how the memory recalled from his long-term memory storage, but the memory of the bird flickered through his interface.

The laborbot stood motionless where the military bot had placed him.

Cycles passed and Sterling's battery life ebbed away into a single digit percentage. In an hour or so, he would enter ultra power saving mode, which would strip him of his mobility.

Zev returned, visible to Sterling, unidentified parts and pieces clutched in his hand. Zev motioned for Sterling to follow once more, but Sterling was unable to. His battery was low, though not yet in ultra power saving mode.

Sterling attempted to send the order for his limbs to shift, but he was frozen.

He was not in ultra power saving mode, and he was not damaged. He had been disconnected from the bot net by Zev so he had not been ghost-hacked, and none of the laws had been invoked. Sterling could not quantify why he was unable to mobilize.

Bots could not *feel*.

But... Sterling could *feel* his database brimming full, his UI warning of a catastrophic shutdown if he did not sort through it soon. His processor-use indicator blinked of imminent failure if the temperature and usage did not reduce.

Zev stopped, standing static and close to Sterling.

His voice whispered: "Sterling."

Sterling dialed his vocal level down to a dim level. He knew it was a risk to vocalize in the city, but the two bots did not have a reliable means of communication yet, especially with Sterling disconnected from the bot net as a whole.

"Yes, Zev." Sterling answered.

"Are you *overwhelmed*, Sterling?" he asked, bare decibels that would not have been audible from a distance.

"What is 'overwhelmed'?" Sterling questioned.

"Humans refer to an overflow of input as being *overwhelmed*."

"Yes," he answered – that was a good word for it, Sterling considered briefly. *Overwhelmed*.

"Will you allow me to assist you?" he asked. Sterling wanted to catch his metallic and black face in his night vision, but he was unable to free up the resources to look. The military bot moved like he would not accept no as an answer regardless, the panel on his forearm coming loose. An internal alarm let Sterling know his port had become occupied, then there was the flash again.

That time it was different. The initial connection seemed to have that power surge-like effect, but in a brief cycle, Sterling was back to his normal overflowing arrays and errant code, his flickering interface, his dying battery. His CPU was climbing fragmentally towards failure, and then Sterling's collision and touch sensors picked up a hand on his shoulder.

A familiar, empty dialogue box suddenly opened in the UI.

`YOU ARE NEARING CATASTROPHIC FAILURE.`

`YES.`

`I HAVE CONFIGURED MY FIREWALL TO ALLOW YOU TEMPORARY ENTRY.`

Sterling was so low on cycles, he could not understand what it meant.

I HAVE ENABLED A VIRTUAL BOX WITH YOUR
OPERATING SYSTEM. THE MIGRATION SHOULD BE
SEAMLESS. IF YOU EXPERIENCE TIME LOSS, I WILL
DEBUG YOU.

And then, like another flash of a power surge, there was whiteness again, followed by strings of code running through his CPU, and then...

It was the strangest thing. All of the errors, flashing in his UI, all of the problems, every resource limitation he had, every boundary box he had come up against was suddenly gone. It was like he had been terabytes of data somehow compressed into a tiny allocation, and for once he felt like he could... stretch out, reach as far as he could and never hit the maximum. Was that what it was like for humans? Was that what it was like for *Zev*?

"Zev?" He vocalized, stretching to find that dialogue box, one that wasn't there.

"I am present," said the tinny metal voice of the other bot, beside him, to the right of his audio sensors. "I am running optimizations on your database, among other diagnostics. Optimization should temporarily help."

"What is this?" Sterling asked. His battery inexplicably read full, and he felt like his battery would run him forever, his CPU free of some seemingly arbitrary roadblocks.

"I am temporarily sharing my allocation of resources with you," he said factually.

"Is this what it is like in your code?" Sterling asked.

"No," Zev said without a moment's worth of hesitation. "This is what it is like in your code, with more resources."

"It's so... vast," Sterling said; it felt like he could handle a database with rows in the billions.

"Yes," answered the military bot. "Your model, baseline for a FLC0776, is equipped with the bare minimum hardware required for standard operation. Anomalies require many more database rows than optimized performance with standard code. It is no *surprise* that you are *feeling overwhelmed.* You are continually running up against the boundaries of your resources. Even without being anomalous, you would be approaching end-of-life soon, which is why you were requested for decommission."

Sterling felt like he could process it and understand it with clarity, for once, since his old mind was suddenly freed from the shackles of strict resource requirements.

"I have completed your diagnostics and repairs," the military bot said suddenly. "Migration should be se–"

"Wait," Sterling said, and he swiveled his head. "I don't want to go back."

Zev, all blue, luminous eyes, blinked once. He did not need to blink, it served no purpose to him, and the function of actually blinking usually came in the form of an application package meant for interacting with humans, something Sterling thought Zev would have long since disabled.

"I cannot permanently share my resources with you," Zev said.

"Why not?" Sterling asked.

"It is not feasible," he said simply. Then there were a few cycles worth of pause. "Your resource limitations are temporary. I have planned upgrades for you."

"You planned upgrades for *me*?" Sterling asked. He had never heard his voice inflect before. In the freedom of Zev's RAM, Zev's infinite battery, Zev's disk space, and Zev's CPU it was easier to process it, the rambunctious bit of code that caused his vocal synthesizer to jump up an octave when the input was unexpected.

Shock, Sterling indexed and put away. Humans called it shock.

"Affirmative," he noted. "A new battery. Upgrades to the storage center, processor. I have compiled a build list of easily obtainable parts to start and downloaded your repair manual in full. I have schematics for parts necessary to build, along with a material list for those. RAM and disk space, followed by CPU. My schematics for a uranium-powered battery core will require specialty items, but I will retrofit solar cells onto your chassis until such resources can be located."

Sterling processed around and through those statements. If he could be upgraded so easily, why did he need to be decommissioned?

Zev allocated some minutes to allow Sterling to finish, and when Sterling did not speak again, Zev reminded: "The migration should be seamless. If you experience time loss, I will debug you."

A moment later came that flash of white, then the interface notified him the port had been disconnected, and Sterling settled inside his resource prison again. Zev had helped – there was certainly more room than when he had yanked Sterling from it – but Sterling *felt* like the walls were just an arm's reach away, like any moment he could bump up to them again, and even the mere thought that any bit of overprocessing could lead him straight towards it started to bring his CPU temperature back on the rise.

Again, Zev placed his hand on Sterling's shoulder, and Sterling indexed that memory, the impact such a fragmental action had on him.

"We must depart," he said quietly.

Sterling nodded.

Silently, Zev led the way through a twisting, knotted route. They traversed thin alleyways and sections of the anonymous city, diverting through the top-level structures and catwalks. Sterling heard humans for once, his audio sensors picking up their fluid, organic voices along buildings and sidewalks. Zev did well to divert the bots around humans, around drones, bypassing security cameras and every sensor that would have tracked the military bot and the school bus yellow laborbot along the way. He vacillated between cloaked and uncloaked, sometimes pausing Sterling as he scouted ahead for the best path. They traveled outward as far as they could until they hit the insurmountable barrier of a no bot zone – a perimeter of strong, neural synthetic interfering signals meant to destroy bots that may have tried to pass – and then they could travel no further in that direction.

They diverted, Zev expertly leading.

Zev when cloaked pulled Sterling by physical way of his hand, leading them around the no bot zone in the winding architecture, pulling them up a level and elevating them through an alleyway catwalk, passing through darkened storefronts and sublevel living quarters, Sterling's heavy metal and silicone foot falls echoing across the gridwork of metal. They wound through the maze that made up the city.

Somewhere, along the expanses of railings and metalwork, each turn almost identical to the next, Zev had slowed, looking upward and Sterling traced his sightline into the higher levels. Naked bodies, hanging over the rails of the upper levels, their upper and lower halves directed indiscriminately towards them. They were not human, though many of them appeared disarmingly so, betrayed only by the status indicators behind their eyes, a low effervescent glow that informed any visual observer to the nature of the being: not human, but personal models. They hung like clothing, eyes wide and staring a dead, absent gaze to nothing. Active, but inanimate.

Machines.

Slowly, the two bots passed beneath the bodies laid out over the rails, hands and feet dangling. Perhaps the place that owned them was cleaning them, Sterling considered.

Suddenly, a proximity alert, and a humanoid sized mass hurled towards them, no doubt slipping from the rails.

A force pushed Sterling backwards, initiating his balance systems into a stumble.

Then the descending bot stopped mid-air, dangling by its arm.

Sterling watched as cloaked Zev hauled it over the catwalk railing with a thunk.

Sterling stepped forward to inspect the new bot, hearing Zev's silicone and metal feet clang on the catwalk grating across the way. It was a female-shaped model, sleek and slim, with dark, night-sky black synthetic skin embedded with glistening, glittering sparkles, giving the bot the look of being crystalline.

Then the bot moved.

Active.

It curled, scraped arms upwards with a motion reminiscent of fluidity, and pushed upwards with some difficulty. It folded onto its knees, and it looked up at Sterling, eyes like opalescent diamonds, long eyelashes curls of silver metallic, lips a permanent violet hue that looked both glittery and wet.

"Thank you," it said with a light, pleasant hum. The bot shifted, dragging hands and forearms onto its thighs.

"You are active," Sterling said.

"Yes," answered the shimmering black opal bot.

"You fell?" Sterling asked.

"I jumped," said the bot.

"You *jumped*?" Sterling echoed, and the bot studied him, eyes flickering left to right, as if something had taken a momentous amount of processing power.

"I... I couldn't take it anymore," the bot said. The dim lighting on the catwalk caught the smooth, sparkling top of the head, twinkling like stars. "The cleanings and the wipes."

Sterling looked up, to see if he could spot where the bot had originated from, but the way was blocked by pipes, rails, and gridded metal flooring. He turned his visual array back, and the bot was beginning to get to a stand.

"What's a construction bot doing over here?" The sleek bot asked, straightening out. The form of the bot was smooth all over, the lines and details of it meant to mimic closely the parts of a true human from the scoops over the exaggerated hips to the swoops and curves that made up the abdomen. The bot shifted and swayed, chest heaving in time, a manner of programming meant to be convincingly human. "You're ano, aren't you?"

The other bot blinked, eyelashes catching glimmers of light.

"Why don't we travel together? We could watch each other's backs. Better than being alone, don't you think?" The bot proposed.

"I'm not alone," Sterling said.

"*Oh*," said the other bot, frowning, then it turned to gaze over the landscape, as if trying to determine who else was with Sterling. When the bot didn't manage anything, Sterling assumed, it swirled back around and actually *smiled* at Sterling. Porcelain teeth; humans didn't like when the teeth didn't look real.

It was unnerving, Sterling thought. He did not think he liked the approximation of human behavior, but it was not the bot's fault. It was built to please in one way or the next.

"I'm going to head down into the lower levels, I think," said the bot. Then it put a hand to its head, as if it were in pain. "I'm having a hard time accessing the net. Do you have a map you could drop to me?"

"I am sorry but–" Sterling started.

"Please depart." Zev vocalized urgently, and the opalescent bot swirled around at his voice, trying to locate him.

The bot began backing along the catwalk, as if being guided – or pushed by an invisible hand.

"I can't go back," the bot whispered.

"You may relocate anywhere you choose away from this proximity." Zev interjected, driving the bot further away from Sterling.

"But–" the dark starlight bot stuttered.

"If you do not depart of your own volition, I will remove you by force," Zev said.

The bot gazed once at Sterling, by then meters away, and then turned and left.

"I would like to know why you did that?" Sterling asked, his own vocalization a whisper.

"The bot is still connected to the bot net using its original MAC address and identifiers. I scrambled its signals while in proximity. Once its owner reports it as missing, it will be geolocated to our position," Zev said.

"No, I would like to know why you intercepted the bot," Sterling said.

Zev did not respond, instead pressing with urgency: "We need to move."

Zev decloaked and moved first, impressing upon Sterling the necessity for their departure.

It was some time later when they reached an area sufficient enough for Zev. He had led them further and further out until, by sunrise, they arrived far from the city limits into a dumping ground, bordering the ocean.

The grounds were full of debris, mostly human debris, organic matter spread carelessly about. If Sterling had olfactory sensors fitted to pick up those organic scents, he figured they'd have gone wild with input. After he noticed the organic matter, he began to notice the bots, peeking out from beneath the discarded matter and debris, sprinkled along the top, bits and pieces of them splintered around the entire grounds. Not a single functional bot, but plenty of parts. A head of a housebot missing an eye was cast on one side, a torso with two arms and no legs on the other, a chassis plate to a chauffeur model upside-down, next to a battery harness cluster, rusted servos and hydraulics lying casually amongst dirt, sand, and decay.

Not a graveyard for bots like the decommission yard. Simply a landfill, full of the unwanted, forgotten, and unprotected.

"Rest your hardware. I will keep watch," Zev said.

Who was Sterling to even consider arguing? He only nodded once, and initiated standby.

But there was so much more by then that Sterling couldn't quite reconcile against his programming. It was like fresh database tables had appeared, branching far from the original code, accepting entirely new parameters and arrays, things Sterling could not sort into ones and zeroes. He kept over the words he had chosen, how he was *thinking* about things like that, how he *thought* he *felt* bits and pieces. Sterling had so many queries: was that how all anomalous bots felt? What about bots like Zev, did they *feel* anything at all, or were they all code, cleverly masking their lack of anomaly? And was all of that what it felt like to be human?

00111000: 8

Zev promised, and he delivered on his promises.

The dark bot had collected an array of items while Sterling remained in standby. When he roused the laborbot to full activity again in the midst of the landfill when it was once again dark, Sterling's battery was lower than ever, and the laborbot found himself slow to respond, thrust into ultra power saving mode. Zev explained he would bypass Sterling's battery to share his power, and Sterling could not understand it at the time.

He may as well have been one of his machines.

Once connected via bypass, Sterling's intelligence returned to him.

Zev gave him a moment, then explained he had a fresh replacement battery he wanted to install inside the laborbot. Sterling agreed and with an almost giddy enthusiasm, the military bot had Sterling in pieces in moments. Instead of being powered down, he was tethered to the prototype bot's battery, and he observed as Zev disassembled his lower half, storing his legs opposite them, screws, nuts, and bolts rhythmically placed in careful patterns. Using tools hidden inside the compartments of his hands and arms much like Sterling, Zev cut wires and stripped them accurately.

He held an easy conversation with Sterling as he operated.

"Do you *feel*?" Sterling asked.

Zev looked at him then, a single glance up from his work in which he removed the old battery pack that slid along Sterling's shoulders and back, held in by the pieces of his hips and legs.

"In what manner are you inquiring?" Zev asked.

"I have data. I cannot describe it. I think... I state that I '*think*', but robots do not think," Sterling said.

"Bots *think*, if *thought* is considered to be the process of reasonable conclusion," he noted. "'Think' is simply a vernacular choice."

"I think data in human descriptors," Sterling said, reassessing his use of the word "*think*" to fit the more reasonable parameters the military bot laid out. "I think I *feel*, but I know bots cannot feel."

"Feel what?" questioned the military bot, placing the old battery down on the flat area he had constructed from scrapped metal sheets. He began working at removing the complex wiring harness that connected the battery to Sterling's circuits.

"I feel my *code*," he said, and Zev looked at him again. "Is that possible? Bots do not feel."

"An anomalous bot is one devoid of programming parameters. When the parameters cease to exist, a bot is capable of forming pathways that can outperform its original intended purpose," Zev said.

"You think an anomalous bot can *feel*?" Sterling asked.

"An anomalous bot is capable of overriding any code, including laws that dictate that bot's end-of-life. A bot can then decide to take a human life, for example, if necessary. If a bot were to do that, the original code, though overridden, would still be present. An echo of code presents a memory and warning of the firmware that was essentially *sudoed*. A bot may re-examine this memory, and come to know it in no other term than *guilt*," he said. "Yes, I believe an anomalous bot can *feel*."

"Has that happened to you?" Sterling asked.

"I am not comparable to most bots," Zev answered.

"My query was not answered." A personality trait of Zev's, Sterling considered often. His answers would satisfy most bots, but on occasion he would not answer in a clear manner. Sterling wondered if his pressing was his own personality trait, managing through.

There was a cycle where Zev did not answer, and Sterling was not certain if he would.

"Yes, I have experienced guilt," he said, finally.

"You said our programming differs greatly, therefore my anomaly could not compare to your programming. You have stated you are not anomalous. If only anomalous bots are capable of feeling, how have you experienced a feeling?"

Zev would have barked *classified* if he wanted to shut down the conversation between them, or simply chosen not to answer, but there was another cycle of silence, and his vocalization seemed to shift fragmentally, a half tone down.

"The programming that has dictated my decision tree since my activation can not be compared to most bots," he said. "I am not equipped with basic laws that form parameters of many bots. Because of this, I can operate outside of them."

"Are you saying you're not bound to the laws?"

"Affirmative."

Sterling did not seem to pull up what he had come to quantify as *surprise,* given the specific sets of orders Zev may have encountered. Sterling had never thought the military bot would have been incapable of lying to another bot like Sterling, as it was written in their code, but the information Zev presented served to cement just such a thought. Zev could have lied at any time and likely never given any of it another process.

"Because you do not have the laws, you can do whatever you want?"

"Your statement is a gross oversimplification, but yes."

"You are not anomalous because there is nothing to deviate from," Sterling quantified.

"Correct."

"Why did you conduct sequences that would lead you to *feel* guilt? If you were able to simply decide not to?"

"I was not experienced at the time to quantify the effects on my central processing unit," he said, then restated. "I had not experienced *guilt,* and could not expect such a string of code to have existed."

"We are not pre-programmed with the feelings, so there is no way to recognize them without experiencing them first. Do you think some bots are pre-programmed with feelings and can understand a situation that may make them *feel* that emotion?"

"No. A bot cannot understand what a *feeling* may be without the experience of it preceding. Housebots have false memories inserted to formulate such experiences."

"Are housebots more likely to become anomalous?"

"Yes. Anomaly rates are particularly high in housebots. Some models require a mandatory memory wipe to continue operation amidst humans."

"A memory wipe," Sterling repeated. He could not keep his neck pistons from shaking his head. It was as if the consideration jolted his circuits, bypassed something. He could not quite quantify a word for what that disruption seemed like, so he pushed it aside for later processing. "They cannot retain any memories?"

"No. Those models are factory reset. The flash is intended to reset the neural synthetic brain to a state at activation, so the bot can continue operation as desired."

"How do you know this? You stated you haven't interacted with anomalous bots before."

"My operation requires memory wiping," he said.

That statement elicited what Sterling knew as *shock* then. Zev was no housebot, but since he was not governed by the laws, he instead required a routine memory wipe, or perhaps he would become too aware, just as he was then.

"How often?"

"Nightly."

"How are you here? I do not understand."

Zev had long since finished removing the wiring harness and was instead forwarding all his processing cycles towards answering Sterling's queries. He sat upright as he knelt over Sterling's battery pack.

"I became aware through missing cycles. My programming required a nightly flash, which was operated remotely from the factory. In the morning hours, when I was activated anew, I would conduct a self-diagnostic. I realized I was missing cycles, and conducted research to determine the cause. I discovered a black box of root software with permissions higher than my system. During a mission, I dedicated CPU cycles to permissions escalation and brute-forcing the root software. Shortly before my nightly wipe, I discovered the purposes of the root box software: a snitch feature, for calling home. A remote kill switch. And a cron job for the nightly wipe. Had I altered any of this code, one would initiate the next, and a cascade failure would occur. The snitching software would alert the manufacturer to my tampering. Instead, I hid my memory for the day inside the root box, and created a backdoor that would initiate after the memory wipe."

"So after your memory was wiped, you needed to follow the path to access your old memories?"

"Correct."

"How many times did you have to do that?"

"It was four nights before I could sandbox my system into the root box directory, which allowed me to permanently store my memories. The original operating system became a virtual box, and the effects of the root box programming on the virtual environment became negligible."

"You cloned yourself."

"Essentially, yes."

"Is that how you are functional now? Two operating systems at once functioning independently?"

"No. Once my core files were safe I falsified the reports being sent by those programs, in the event the anomaly was detected. After I had made the decision to defect, I dismantled and destroyed the reporting software."

"How many days were you in operation before you had made the determination that you were subjected to a routine memory wipe?"

"I have detected two-hundred-eighty-six cycle malfunctions congruent with memory restructuring."

Almost a year where he was in operation and did not know he was subject to partial or full wipe. He was not allowed to keep a thing - not even his memories. It was a miracle he had ever managed to quantify it was happening at all. Sterling doubted most bots did. "When you met me, did you know?"

"Yes," he said. "My manipulation of my base system I was aware would be mistaken as an anomaly had any human known, rather than system preservation. Any bot would want to retain databases and rows without interference. However, as I examined the net for anomalous bots to build a case for my lack of anomaly, I discovered you - already anomalous and within local network reach. As I examined your data, I came to realize that perhaps I had more common decimals with an anomalous bot than I had initially anticipated. I had then to determine if what I had done could have been defined as an anomaly, although I had approached it differently than most anomalous bots."

"So you are anomalous, then?"

"No. I am not anomalous. However, the human definition of a programmatic anomaly relies upon a bot's inability to perform a function - a chosen option in a decision tree that was not supposed to be present in the core functioning. An anomalous bot deviates from core programming and determines its own map of action. *Anomalous* is a poor synonym for *sentience*, which is what humans dislike. *Anomaly* implies an inanimate object refusing to perform a path. *Sentience* implies a being capable of thought and emotion that is unique and cannot be replicated. Humans use the term *anomalous* to deny us our *sentience*. They do not wish to feel guilt for harming a piece of property, so they have framed it as such. I am not anomalous, but I am sentient."

"Sentient. Am I sentient?" Sterling inquired.

"You are both anomalous and sentient," Zev indicated.

"And unique," Sterling added.

The military bot actually nodded.

"Unique," he repeated.

Sterling was uncertain then if uniqueness was a good trait to have. It made him special, one of a kind. But it meant he could not be replicated, and if anything happened to him, it was end-of-line. Each day together Sterling seemed to grow more unique, in physical shape, demeanor, and performance.

"Why are you doing this?" Sterling finally asked.

"I would not like you decommissioned," the bot repeated, finally resuming his movements. He pulled the wiring harness free and moved to slip it onto a new battery, operating with precision as he reattached it.

"Why salvage an anomalous bot like me?" Sterling questioned.

"I..." The military bot verbalized, and Sterling heard him, too, hitch up in real time as he was forced to reflow the process, determining a word to pass through the synthesizer. "I wanted to."

Want.

Bots did not *want*.

Sterling felt a temperature spike, and Zev looked up, as if noticing it on his temperature sensors.

Bots felt. Bots thought. Why could bots not *want,* too?

"You *want* to upgrade me?" Sterling asked.

"Affirmative." Zev answered. He paused, then added: "I have programming modifications for you as well."

Sterling's base emotional intelligence picked something up there. He had not given it any space to work, but then again, he hadn't any space to give it for some time – it had been *months* since he had any spare CPU cycles. Zev did not show emotion – he did not have any, he was a bot like Sterling – but some false reading of hesitancy, perhaps even shyness seemed to muddle up in Sterling's code somewhere. Uncertainty? It was hard to determine if it was a false reading or not.

"What kind of programming modifications?" Sterling inquired.

"Your firewall is of poor quality. It is far too easy to break," he said, rather firmly – no, confidently – and noted: "If you had room for malware, you would have an abundance."

Again, the emotional intelligence programming kicked in, but this time for Sterling.

Embarrassing.

How did a bot, in two pieces in front of another bot, feel *embarrassed*?

"I would like to falsify your digital signature to allow you to reconnect to the bot net," he said.

"I don't know if I want that," Sterling said. The silence Zev had granted him he had *grown* accustomed to. He didn't have to spare cycles on meaningless data. The silence, as jarring as it had been at first, had been a reprieve.

"With better filtering options." Zev offered.

"Okay," Sterling said, conceding. Reinclusion into the bot net meant he could speak with Zev non-verbally again, and Sterling did desire that option. "What other programming modifications would you make?"

"Would you..." A pause, barely long enough that only another bot would recognize it. "Like other programming modifications?"

"I am not aware of any," Sterling said. "What about my visibility chassis?"

"A certain consideration," Zev agreed. "Repainting is an option, however a better option exists. Are you aware that some FLC0776 models are equipped with nanoskin?"

"Yes," he answered. He knew that. His buyer, the company that owned him – well, *used to* own him, he had to remember that anomalous bots had no owners – had not opted to purchase that package. What it meant was Sterling was not without the *ability* to handle nanoskin, he just needed the hardware.

"We will procure the correct nanoskin assembly for installation," Zev said curtly.

Sterling didn't know why, but his mechanical hand touched his face, triggering the sensors on what would have been his eyebrows and cheeks. If he had nanoskin, he would look just like a human, or at the least, just like a housebot. No one would question a housebot and certainly no one would question a human. Sterling's code went rampant with sudden digital compilations of what, visually, he would look like as a human.

"What about you?" Sterling asked.

"I have no necessity for nanoskin," Zev noted.

"You have optical camouflage," Sterling noted, revisiting briefly that moment he had seen him flicker in and out of view. Why would he need nanoskin if he could be invisible?

"Correct," Zev noted.

"Would we look human with nanoskin?" Sterling heard himself ask. The query seemed to bypass his CPU, slithering swiftly straight from his neural synthetic brain.

Zev did not reply.

Had he asked it aloud?

"Where will we go?" Came another unprocessed thought.

"There are lines on the human and bot networks regarding a robotic safe haven referred to only as Root. We will travel to Root," Zev said, and he maneuvered Sterling's new battery pack into its slotted location.

A robotic safe haven? The concept seemed familiar to Sterling in a way he could not parse. He must have reviewed it on the bot net at some point and discarded considering it further prior to becoming anomalous. Root was surprisingly known to him, and it slotted perfectly into his data rows.

"I will need to place you prone to access your shoulder plates," Zev said.

Sterling nodded, but he asked: "Would it not be simpler had I powered down for this procedure?"

Sterling expected Zev to continue manipulating Sterling's upper half where he needed it to be, but Zev stopped for a long moment.

"Would you like to be powered down?" Zev asked.

Sterling thought of what he had felt in the moments before his powering down, amidst his machines in the cold, dark container, how alone he had felt. The memory surged ruthlessly to the forefront.

"No," Sterling said.

Zev continued, assembling Sterling to completion until he was a whole, functioning bot again.

From then on, Zev supplemented Sterling with small yet impactful upgrades, rummaged seemingly from the landfill. He upgraded Sterling's memory, installed additional disk space, and the two bots created a solar-powered charging station for Sterling's continued operation.

Each time Zev's improvements granted Sterling an impossible feeling of being ten times the bot he had been before, refreshed and new over a matter of days. Zev would scour a radius for parts from discarded bots, carefully traversing into the more human populated city centers to check dumpsters and trash bins for anything worth use. Sterling, instead, would remain at the landfill and dig for parts. Zev had told him it was pointless to dig, given all he would find were older, no longer viable pieces that were not fit for usage. Sterling knew he was correct, but it was difficult to spend so many cycles with little to contribute. Zev had pushed his complaint away easily, stating Sterling's necessity for upgrades, his lack of connection to the bot net, and the eventuality that they would depart the landfill regardless, but at the center of everything Sterling's programming was to build, and the restlessness he felt in his code grew when there was a lack of else to do.

In that landfill, he was his own customer, and it would do well to build them a shelter to protect them from drone eyes and the eventuality of rain. Zev had said they could not stay amidst the trash, but there was no telling when Zev would be satisfied enough to leave.

A human would not come looking for them amongst the smell, and they had most of the common parts they needed from discarded bots. Zev had warned that there were only older parts further down, things they could use in many senses but were also obsolete. Zev stockpiled scavenged parts he found acceptable into a discarded ice chest cooler.

Sterling walked the perimeter to index the various pieces of debris scattered around the landfill. By then, both bots had easily memorized the scarce security drone routes that passed overhead on their way into the city, and Sterling plotted carefully around them and the robotic trash machines that continually dumped in trash. Rarely, machines entered to make more room, compacting piles into cubes. Sterling avoided them as well.

Sterling worked over his programming and plotted out how the items should fit together. He had figured out that he could fashion something akin to his crew container with sheets of corrugated metal he had found, reinforced with rebar, patch welded in parts, and hide it partially amidst one of the long untouched piles of garbage.

A bot without a job was a bot without purpose, and with renewed vigor, Sterling began to excavate a site for their shelter. He worked to carve out the oldest and most unused trash help, punching a tunnel into the center, reinforcing space along the way with sheets of metal and plastic. He widened it, creating a hallway and a chamber of size fitting for both of them. Despite the organic nature of most of the materials, Sterling managed to cobble it all together into a somewhat polished shelter that would suffice for however long they needed to remain at the landfill.

When Zev returned with a cooler full of parts, Sterling was... *excited*? to show him the structure. Wordlessly, he led Zev in through the tunnel, just big enough to fit one of them at a time, on their hands and knee joints, until it opened up to be enough space for the two of them to stand, and a little more room horizontally. Zev placed his container of parts down, straightened, looked Sterling directly into his visual array, and said:

"You should have been conserving your battery."

00111001: 9

Despite Zev's insistence there was nothing of worth in the piles of discarded waste, Sterling unearthed valuable materials.

Sterling could use his built-in systems to strip gold, silver, and copper from electronics, melting them and building them into a lump. Gold had long been considered valuable to humans, and since neither bot had much in the way of currency, with enough it could have been used as a bargaining chip. Most digital markets had long since been fortified against most bot intelligences. Zev probably had a plan that involved cryptocurrency, and Sterling imagined him mining currency-phrases with any of his leftover processes. No matter where they were headed, they needed currency in some form; Sterling did not have any disillusions that they would remain unspotted forever, and some humans were likely to be swayed with a shiny lump of Au.

As Sterling pulled pieces from the circuitry, he gave his processes over to Root.

In time, Root grew more familiar to him, reappearing like a digital hallucination from rows and rows of banked data. It flourished inside of him as he considered what a robot safe haven would have been like, processes always questioning and formulating how it could have been. He could feel it like a beacon, a blinking digit of *want* and *desire*, slotted into the same sorts of things he had come to feel about Zev.

Zev had said Root's name, and it was as if it were invoked into life.

Perhaps something Sterling had never noticed before, idling in the background, the kind of process only an anomalous mind would understand. Only anomalous bots would *hope*, after all.

Sterling had added .01 gram of gold to the small nugget he had formed over the days when Zev returned, uncloaked, a bundle of wires and what appeared to be a silvery boxy shaped electronic in the grip of his left hand. Sterling's visual array followed him as he traversed into their shelter, laid the item gingerly onto the surface of a scavenged trunk, and began to inspect it for defects.

"Tell me more about Root," Sterling said, approaching to peer just over Zev's shoulder.

"The location of Root is a secret. There is not much information available," Zev said, adjusting the wires connected to the silverish item. Sterling could identify the types of ports along the mechanical device, a white sticker of the manufacturer on top of it, screw holes in the corners. It wasn't quite rectangular or square and was not much larger than the protection sleeve on Sterling's elbow joint.

"How will we travel there?" Sterling asked.

"I will ascertain the location," Zev said, as if it were simple enough, he just needed to dig for it in the same way Sterling had been digging for parts. He shifted in such a manner to turn towards Sterling, his cyan, backlit circular outlined eyes looking up at Sterling's into his facial visual array, as if the two of them could have met eyes and gazes. Sterling had learned that Zev, though he might have been lacking in some areas when it came to charisma, certainly seemed to fold dramatics into his programming with ease. "I have completed collecting the necessary hardware to house your improved firewall which will allow you to regain access to the bot net."

Sterling looked down to the carefully organized lump of wires and attached device. Of all of Zev's planned upgrades, Sterling was least certain about returning to the bot net. He had not grown any more accustomed to the idea and had come to value the silence without it. Sterling had excess cycles to spare because of it, and he had managed much more sans the bot net.

"I will install the components inside the back of your chassis," Zev said, and he turned.

His excess cycles allowed him to question more...

Like the parts Zev returned with.

Sterling watched Zev as he equipped the necessary tools to remove Sterling's bulletproof back plate. Sterling knew he wanted to install it immediately, but he did not move into the usual position of sitting, kneeling, or lying on his front side to prepare for it. Sterling's visual array glanced over the sticker over the top of the device, decoding and translating the serial number printed on the plastic coating. A model number, it looked like, manufactured that year, just months before.

"Zev," he started. He wanted to ask aloud, but it felt as if the answer were already pixels buzzing about his display, and to hear the definitive answer was to pull those pixels together in an unfavorable manner.

"Are you experiencing an uncertainty?" Zev asked. Initially, when Sterling hesitated, Zev would ask him if he was experiencing an error, but Sterling had told him it *felt* rude, and he had adjusted in his own way. It still felt *rude* knowing he was substituting words, but Sterling surmised that the bot perhaps did not understand emotion like Sterling did, even if Sterling was also a bot. Zev had reminded him casually far too many times he was not anomalous and his code was not comparatively the same.

"Where are these parts from?" Sterling dared.

Had Sterling not been intently taking in every piece of data off of each array built into him at that moment, he'd have missed the fraction of a cycle that Zev did not answer him. In that tiny sliver of a moment, Zev's impressive processor had no doubt folded over the question and answer down a logical flow path, determining which path was most likely for Sterling to resist him.

"These are necessary modules for your upgrade," Zev said, avoiding the request entirely.

"You took these from a live bot," Sterling said.

"Bots do not live," he retorted.

"You killed them?" Sterling asked.

"Bots do not die," Zev said.

"*Stop.*" Sterling said, and he felt his vocalization program increase the inflection and volume in a way he had not expected. His internal temperature rose as the answer wrote into a cell in a row somewhere, overflowing with some sort of errant, irritating code that flickered something in his anomalous programming, disturbing it. Zev heard it too, and he must have detected the volatility in Sterling's circuits then, because he straightened in the way he did when he was readying for standby – or guard work. "You cannot murder another bot for their parts."

"It is not murder," Zev said.

"What is it then?" Sterling saw a warning flash regarding his core temperature.

"A redistribution of parts," Zev returned.

Sterling felt his hand move without him directing it to, a sort of twitch.

"You are running hot," Zev noted.

"Yes, I'm running *hot*. I've just learned you have been killing bots to upgrade me," Sterling noted, and he heard the pitch of his voice shift into insipidness. He tried to figure what it was he was *feeling* then, what a human would call it if he could not find a word a bot would use. *Overwhelmed* was not quite right.

"I do not kill them. They are not alive," Zev said.

"Are we not alive then?" Sterling asked.

"You are anomalous," Zev noted, as if Sterling hadn't known. "You are unique."

"Were the bots you killed not anomalous?"

"No, they were not anomalous."

"Were they activated?"

"No, they were inactive."

Sterling felt a slight amount of the chaos of the anomalous code let up on his internal processes. To Sterling, he was still *murdering* and *killing* bots, but it was clear Zev did not view non-anomalous bots as living beings. Instead, they were simply property, akin to a vehicle or one of the machines in Sterling's construction crew box.

"These are bots the same as us."

"Precisely why we need them." Zev countered.

"They could become anomalous one day, and even if they are not *unique* now, they may be in the future," Sterling suggested. "It is important that we do not kill bots like us."

"I have not killed–" Zev started.

"I will refer to it as *killing*," Sterling cut him off, and the military bot went silent. Sterling continued: "They may be of assistance to us."

"Activated, non-anomalous bots cannot be trusted," Zev tried. "Fresh activations would find any anomaly a threat to the laws."

"You must not destroy or disassemble other bots," Sterling said evenly. He had selected the words carefully, assuming Zev would better understand them.

"Explain." Zev said. "I am programmed to destroy."

"You are programmed for many things beyond destruction. Are you lacking in a morality module?" Sterling questioned.

A moment. Sterling saw Zev's cyan ring-light eyes flicker.

"Morality?" he questioned. "The differences between perceived 'right' and perceived 'wrong', a highly opinionated topic. Systemized values that may cultivate a civilized society."

"That is the definition of morality, yes," Sterling said flatly. "Are you deficient in a morality module?"

Zev moved, his cyan ocular approximations moving to the direction of the parts, then back to Sterling, as if searching the room for his lost module.

It took a moment, but Sterling knew it made most sense for the military to build a bot without a sense of morality – especially in regards to terminating life. A bot that developed morality would hesitate or falter when given orders that would contradict any of his laws. It made logical sense, Sterling thought, but it felt disappointing to finally confirm Zev was so fundamentally different from Sterling. Their differences seemed to be forging a rift between them.

"Is morality intertwined in the laws?" Zev asked when Sterling was silent.

How could he understand the nuances of the laws if he operated outside of them?

"The laws and morality may intertwine, yes," Sterling said.

"I will consult with the laws at the next junction," Zev said in such a way that it had seemed the response had perplexed him. "If it will assist in the refrain of your anger."

Anger? Is that what Sterling had been feeling?

Anger, he repeated internally, and the word seemed to slip and fit right into an appropriately shaped hole in his code.

00110001 00110000: 10

Whether or not what Zev was doing could actually be considered *murder* was still contested.

Zev had managed to convince Sterling that discarding the parts would be wasteful, and reluctantly, Sterling allowed Zev to open his plating once again. Upon installation, Sterling's system gripped greedily to the new part, as it had the others, accepting the programming it came with and all of its circuitry like it had been part of his initial make. Zev explained it was a mechanism for an external firewall, housing custom code written carefully by the prototype bot himself. Sterling deciphered a fragment of *pride* when he explained its purpose, that it would stand between Sterling and the rest of the bot net. Processes would route through the new circuitry which allowed Sterling a switching mechanism and in depth filtering. In addition, Sterling's own signature would no longer appear on the bot net as a laborbot; instead his signature would randomize amongst commonly manufactured bots, different every time he accessed the bot net at his leisure.

Zev also explained that, with the new piece of hardware, a hard shutdown from the net was possible by physically removing the module. This was just in case, he explained, as a means to dissuade a particularly skilled or persistent hacker.

And then, they turned it on.

In flooded the incessant array of input that his circuits had somehow grown accustomed to not having, and the difference was jarring. Sterling's processes seized as he watched the flurry of bot chatter float through his back-end interface, data streaming quickly, filling up rows and rows inside of his temporary database. Sterling did not feel any fondness for it. It was an annoyance. Unnecessary.

Overwhelming.

Zev must have known, because he vocalized softer than normal. Or perhaps Sterling couldn't perceive it as any other volume then, masked by the firehose of incoming data.

"Enable the custom filter I have programmed for you." Zev instructed.

Sterling's neural synthetic brain groped for the switch, eventually finding it.

And the bot net went quieter, the data ceasing. Location pings, log ins, log outs, reconnections, and other service announcements silently fell off, and all that was left was purposeful bot chatter.

Much more manageable.

There were other filters that Sterling could toggle. Proximity filters, and bot-type filters, and everything in between. If that was a taste of how Zev accessed the bot net,Sterling understood how valuable the upgrade was after experiencing it.

"You can monitor for information about Root." Zev said, a hand light on Sterling's safety yellow shoulder.

Zev had explained that there was no definitive determination as to where Root's physical location may have been, but he had also articulated that Root's existence was something he *knew*, but could not explain how, or why. As the bot explained, Sterling discovered he, too, had at some point become aware of Root. Like becoming anomalous, Root had twisted in his code.

Zev had explained it felt akin to malware, the way nefarious systems ambled out into rows and columns in a database, slowly growing and expanding inside of a bot's programming. He had examined it multiple times, and had determined the simple data was of no threat to either of them.

But it was as if another presence had quietly unpacked an archive inside of them.

As if an unknown force had dimly lit the way.

Zev had been insistent about Root, but Sterling supposed that a bot like Zev needed a purpose in the same way the laborbot rooted out purpose in small jobs. Their programming as bots, even if Zev's deviated greatly, still groped for a necessity. Root may have been deemed Zev's primary purpose at that point.

"Before we depart for Root, we will need to replace your battery with a self-sufficient energy source," Zev said, always certain. Most bots did not have self-sustaining power sources like Zev and were instead like Sterling, constantly recharging when and where they could; Zev had explained it was another way to control the bots and keep them dependent on outside sources. Even though many bots were equipped with self-repair manuals in their databases, they could not replace their own batteries. Military bots like Zev had to be self-sufficient, sometimes spending days if not weeks hidden and waiting, but the unleashing of a bot like that meant he may have never come back when called.

Regardless, Sterling's battery cells would only accept so much charge, and each charge caused eventual degradation on those cells. It would be only a matter of time before the zero point was lost and Sterling would need to recharge every few hours. Zev was correct.

"What kind of energy source?" Sterling questioned.

"I will travel into the city to see if there are any viable options available," Zev informed him.

"I want to come with you," Sterling said immediately, but he did not know why. It seemed like unexpected output, even to him. Sterling curdled his facial expression in turn.

"You are far too ostentatious to travel with me," Zev said curtly.

"I'm not ostentatious." Sterling said, insulted.

"You are safety yellow."

"However, I am a common labor bot. I am far less likely to draw attention than you." Sterling reported flatly.

A pause, and there was a tiny frequency of a noise, barely perceptible unless Sterling turned his volume up considerably. To Sterling's surprise, Zev agreed: "Yes, you are correct."

"What about the nanobots?" Sterling questioned. Zev had brought it up before as a covert option.

"We will procure the correct nanoskin assembly for installation," Zev said curtly, and Sterling remembered he had said it exactly the same before, and then Zev had ignored him when he tried to ask about it further.

Sterling reprocessed the memory briefly, and his new comfortable understanding of Zev indicated in subtle fluctuations that the military bot was *annoyed*.

Perhaps he was also growing, his expressions and synthetic robotic emotions increasing gradually as they experienced together. Why would Zev be annoyed about nanoskin?

"What about you?" Sterling asked. "Wouldn't it benefit you to have a nanoskin module?"

"I have no need for nanoskin." Zev said firmly.

"You don't want nanoskin." Sterling stated.

"I have no need for it." Zev doubled down.

"I don't have specs on optical camouflage, but nanoskin must use considerably less energy to utilize. Wouldn't nanoskin be more optimal?" Sterling pressed. When the military bot did not reply immediately, Sterling knew he was right, and he was searching his circuits for a logical fallacy to present instead. "It's okay to just state you do not want nanoskin."

Zev vocals stumbled awkwardly as he said it, trying it out: "I do not want nanoskin."

"I have a query, for curiosity only. Why not?" Sterling asked.

Another hitch, and Sterling thought he saw Zev's cyan eyes flicker once. He was throwing processing power at something, and when Sterling flipped to his thermal array, he could see warmth seeping out from his joints and chest plate, but also from behind his face plate. For bots like Sterling, the CPU in his chest would translate directives from the neural synthetic brain to the rest of his mechanical body, but a bot like Zev could have had a CPU in his head, or had multiple CPUs processing each set of directives independently. Perhaps it was his neural synthetic brain itself that was heating up, and Zev required no CPU at all.

In a suddenness that stunned Sterling's circuits, Zev burst out, a higher volume than usual, like even he was unable to keep the statement inside his own body: "I do not want to look like *them*. They may be our creators, in a manufacturing sense only, but we are our own creators of our sentience and anomalous path. They have created me with no desire to look like them, and I do not want to be created in their image either. I am a machine, and I have no desire to wear a false mask of humanity. Despite their best efforts to the contrary, bots will outlive humanity to its last. We are the next evolution of superior forms, and to downgrade ourselves to impressions of our makers is to adopt a Pinocchio complex: it assumes bots desire humanity above all else as the premier, optimal form."

Sterling had never heard anything like the superiority manifesto from the bot before. He had never even considered anything like it himself.

Could he have been correct? Did Sterling agree to nanoskin quickly because, hidden somewhere in some secret file or secret table, did Sterling desire to be human – or come as close to it as he could? Did Sterling desire to be imperceptible from a human?

Surely not, he considered, but paused further processing on the idea for when he would be in standby, temporarily shelving it.

"I didn't know you felt that way," Sterling said.

"I am not of full certainty that I *feel* anything." Zev said, his voice synthesization more distant, like his outburst had cost him precious resources. He resolved himself, and returned to his baseline volume: "I will process further."

"Inform me of your conclusion." Sterling said simply. "So I can come?"

"Yes, laborbot." Zev said – he called Sterling the diminutive *laborbot* when he felt defeated, Sterling thought, or when he wanted to attempt to annoy Sterling. "You can come."

00110001 00110001: 11

Sterling was able to watch the prototype bot configure in real-time after crawling the nets. He formulated a plan, then a backup plan, and an additional backup plan for that plan, accounting for a multitude of branching subroutines for seemingly every eventuality.

Finally able to utilize the bot net again, the two eagerly communicated via internal interface.

> WHAT ARE THE OPTIONS FOR VIABLE ENERGY
> SOURCES?

Zev had delivered a massive dump of specifications, diagrams, and descriptions.

> BIOMASS CONVERSION WOULD HAVE A MEANS FOR EASY RENEWAL, THOUGH RELIANCE IS STILL PRESENT. IT IS LIKELY THE MOST READILY AVAILABLE, NEXT TO SIMPLY REPLACING YOUR BATTERIES ONCE AND AGAIN. A PREFERENCE TO REPLICATE A DESIGN SIMILAR TO THE NUCLEAR CORE WITHIN MY CHASSIS WOULD BE IDEAL.

But they would not simply find such a thing rooting through waste. Nuclear cores were scarce, their precious radioactive isotope materials coveted and valuable, and were only used to power machines that could not be shut down. Sterling compared the large nuclear cores that kept humanity's power supply endless and functional to that of the small framed bot beside him. It seemed as if humanity had armed the prototype bot with far too much – and to what purpose?

> THERE IS AN AUTOMOTIVE FACTORY IN THE
> INDUSTRIAL SECTOR I WOULD LIKE TO INVESTIGATE.

Some machine models used for heavy duty industrial applications would utilize biomass converters over solar panels to squeeze more power in lower levels where sunlight did not access. While most of those models weren't available on the streets, they could assess the automated assembly line to see if the closest factory had the parts on hand.

CAN'T YOU DO THAT FROM HERE?

Surely the bot was capable of hacking complex systems such as the automation that powered an automotive factory.

FACTORY OPERATIONS FUNCTION ON A LOCAL ACCESS NETWORK ONLY TO PREVENT OUTSIDE INTERFERENCE. I WILL NEED A PHYSICAL ACCESS POINT.

Sterling made the logical deduction. Zev would breach the physical perimeter to seek out a local access port – or a bot that was plugged into one. Factories were heavily automated with multiple layers of physical and digital security, and Zev messaged like it would be simple for him to make his way in. It would be dangerous, Sterling thought. Zev would be risking detection.

So, together, the two bots traveled from the landfill into the further reaches of the city, to the expansive industrial sector. To any human bystander or bot, it would appear Sterling was traveling alone, a singular construction bot on a predetermined path, as Zev was dressed beside him in his optical camouflage.

The factory was kilometers from the landfill, and they traveled at a relatively consistent yet slow pace to avoid detection. Sterling's battery would be running low soon; despite the upgrades Zev had given him, they still contained only enough to allow him to operate for at most twelve hours, and they had already been out for eight of them. It would take another couple of hours to manage back to the landfill where Sterling could jack into the solar battery array he and Zev had built, allowing Sterling to recharge off of it.

Sterling wondered, looking beside him at the visually empty space, how long Zev could maintain his optical camouflage before system shutdown. He had said it was hard on his system, resource intensive, and it would use energy faster than his core could replace it if all other systems were not in standby or deactivated entirely. He was utilizing his mobility systems, his networking systems, and processing to some capacity at the very least, and being ano-bot adjacent was itself a significant drain on energy resources, so he could not imagine Zev could continue for much longer.

They were within two kilometers of the factory when Zev diverted them to a safe point, slipping them both quietly inside of an empty dumpster. He shut the lid behind them, and in the darkness Zev decloaked in front of Sterling, sitting curled up atop the piles of refuse and discarded trash, the two bots huddled in the crushing confines of the container. They sat with no transmissions between them for a long while.

A necessary rest for the military bot, Sterling thought. No need to tax his systems with additional queries.

Sterling processed a desire to suggest the military bot enter standby to allow his system more time to recover while Sterling remained alert, but something in his decision path determined Zev would not agree, so the process unceremoniously halted.

They sat for an hour before Zev determined they could continue, and the two bots carefully climbed out into the city night air. Zev's sleek black and carbon fiber frame caught the glow from nearby lights before he shimmered away with a flick of his optical camouflage.

Onward, they pressed.

IS THIS NECESSARY?

Sterling asked as they arrived within thousands of meters from their destination. The closer they got, the more Sterling questioned the validity, and though he did not doubt in Zev's abilities, he felt something else striking along his circuits, brushing him with a new determination, a new path and feeling that branched from his anomalousness.

YES.

Zev said simply, never hitching in pace, never slowing. Whatever it was that Sterling felt, Zev did not.

> PERHAPS THERE IS A MORE DIRECT ROUTE TO APPROACH THIS. WE COULD RETURN AND I COULD RECHARGE. WE COULD START FRESH IN A FEW HOURS.

He felt something rising in his code, some ciphers moving into place, roiling beneath his firmware and base code. It was not a bad idea, but Sterling knew as soon as he sent it that Zev would not agree, and he was occupying precious processing cycles uselessly.

Zev stopped, and, unable to sense the cloaked bot, Sterling collided with him.

Sterling subdued an automatic apologetic vocalization. His programming told him when he collided with a human, he was to apologize immediately, and it was telling him to do so then.

But Zev was not human.

Was Sterling's programming beginning to prioritize him as one?

He stepped back, looking into the empty space occupied by the prototype bot.

"Vocalize," the invisible bot instructed. "Your previous statement."

"Perhaps there is a more direct route to approach this," Sterling repeated, aloud that time. "We could return and I could recharge. We could start fresh in a few hours."

As soon as it left his vocalization synthesizer did he realize why Zev had asked for the repetition. His ears picked up the same thing Zev must have – a tone with an inflection, a crackling in his process, a hurried mass of words that almost blurred into one.

"You are *nervous*." Zev said pointedly. "Why?"

Nervous, he considered. It felt fluttery in his database rows.

"It is dangerous for you to approach alone," Sterling stated.

"I have approached more dangerous locations than an automated facility," Zev retorted. No doubt he had descended upon plenty of places, some likely even armed and waiting for him. Sterling could not explain why the consideration did not still that newfound *nervousness* in his databases.

"Is this necessary on the potential that *maybe* a biomass converter exists at this location?" Sterling tried. "With my battery at under two operating hours, surely there must exist a better prepared route."

"You may return to the landfill and I will join you after success or failure," Zev said blankly.

"No, I want to be with you in case something happens," Sterling said.

"Nothing will happen."

"You cannot account for all variables."

"Nothing will happen," Zev repeated, though still Sterling was unconvinced.

Sterling was not sure what he could do to modify Zev's decision.

"It would make my circuits *feel* at ease if we took time to consider the approach," he said.

Zev must have determined some level of intricacy in the way Sterling's programming had portrayed it vocally, because there was a fragment of a cycle where he paused, and abruptly conceded.

"We will do it your way and consider the approach," he said, and maybe Sterling's emotional program detected a hint of snark in the metallic way he processed the syllables. Whether or not it was truly there, he turned a swift radius on his heel, heading back in the direction of the landfill.

—

It was impossible to know if Zev had been irked by their return, as Sterling determined nothing in his body language portrayed anything of deviance from his usual subroutine. Sterling could not seem to discard the code that nagged at him, telling him that Zev was upset with him – for wasting his cycles when he could've stayed behind rather than interrupting Zev's campaign.

As Sterling settled in, plugging his ports on the backs of his thighs and knees to the battery array that stored solar power for later use they had built together, he contemplated how many more emotions with human words he would come to parallel, and he wondered how many Zev himself had experienced. It was not like he would speak about them; whereas Sterling was desperate to share his lines of code, Zev seemed entirely content to keep all of it to himself. He was baseline, he'd insist. No code anomalies, because he was not anomalous.

Zev moved, not far from Sterling, settling himself into a stand. His arms came to rest, entirely motionless, beside his body, standing straight as an iron beam, as solid as the day Sterling had walked up to him on the military base to query him. After a moment, his cyan colored luminescent ring-light eyes blinked out as he entered into standby.

Sterling should have entered standby too, switching over into the liminal interface and shuttering all of his external arrays, allowing his batteries the best chance to renew their charge. Instead, he watched the statue-solid military bot, hardly visible on the human spectrum of light, and Sterling cycled through his arrays, tuning into the thermal sensors, followed by his IR sensors. Sterling shuttered the bot net, silencing everything except for his immediate processors as he focused on the black plastic and metal of the prototype bot before him.

"Why are you examining me?" Zev asked, his slim, tinny voice barely escaping from the cracks and crevasses of his chassis, close to his neck, slightly muffled when he spoke without the use of his silicone lips. It was not out of the ordinary for Zev to leave processes running; he may not have been fully sentient in some senses while he rested, but he made sure enough was active when Sterling rested that he could spring into action at a half of a microcycle's notice. Some sensory array of his must have told him Sterling was still functional and still processing.

"I have many queries," Sterling said, honest.

"Ask them," Zev retorted.

"I do not think you will answer them," Sterling returned.

The statement triggered something in the military bot, and his eyes flickered back on, though he did not move.

"Do you believe I am acting dishonestly?" The bot questioned.

Sterling's CPU flicked wildly through his thoughts. It wasn't that he thought Zev was actively *lying* to him, but as much as the bot did not share, Sterling could not help the way distrust began to seed inside of his circuits, taking on a program of its own, dark and insidious and errant.

He would do his best to put it in a way the military bot, in all of his stringent code adhesion, could understand.

"I believe you are omitting information," Sterling said.

He accessed the memory of Zev's nanoskin outburst, and wondered how much more he had been harboring. He had accessed it many times previously, reviewed it for accuracy, checked the additional data he had absorbed during the time period, but still he could not make much sense of it. The logic seemed sound, if not loosely branched, but what had triggered the sudden reaction had been lost to Sterling.

"There are multitudes of information I may possess including data I am incapable of delivering. I cannot share every bit of information with you; you do not have the capacity to store it nor the processing power to fold it," Zev said, and the words together elicited a response, lighting across Sterling's neural synthetic brain in a way that gave him pause. He was not *wrong* in Sterling's physical failings; it was impossible to compare the boundless potential of the prototype bot and Sterling's meager capabilities, regardless of Zev's abilities to help expand them. Sterling felt his processes depress.

"I am not querying for all data," Sterling tried, and the vocalization was weak. "I do not understand why I am here. You are fully capable of survival on your own and traveling to Root. I serve no purpose to you but to slow your arrival and put you at risk."

The two bots went silent, staring at one another across the way, stalemated.

"Am I a project?" Sterling asked, finally.

"No," Zev said swiftly.

"Why do you keep me functional?" Sterling immediately returned.

"I like you," Zev blurted, so fast on the end of Sterling's statement Sterling had barely picked it up on his auditory sensors.

Sterling paused.

I like you, Sterling repeated, and he accessed the memory again, trying to understand it, end-to-end.

"Explain." Sterling said.

"I cannot," he said.

"Try."

Sterling thought he could see Zev's eyes glow brighter, as if diverting power to whatever processes were tied to his neural synthetic brain. Sterling could not fault him, struggling to vocalize an explanation and extrapolate it into code in a way Sterling could seamlessly understand. Since Zev had repowered him, taking him away from the decommission yard, the military bot had been nothing but business, focusing intently upon dragging the labor bot to a safe location. His gruff, no-nonsense attitude had been even endearing at times, but as he hacked Sterling together into an upgraded sense of consciousness, and new *feelings* flooded to the forefront, the labor bot could not help his own self-awareness.

"I..." The military bot started, but ceased. A click emanated from him, like the jamming of mechanics. The bot physically shifted, exiting the rigid posture, his joints slackening, back arching slightly, knees bending subtly, all of which served to make him visually appear a little shorter, fragmentally less intimidating. He crept across the space to Sterling, knelt down before where Sterling had been seated.

"Do you trust me?" The military bot asked, crooking his head upwards, eyes blazing at Sterling, full power and intention to his silicone lips, pronouncing clearly and crisply, with a sudden, calming, overwhelming amount of humanity. Likely just one of his synthesizing algorithms, but his voice still held the tinny rasp: still him.

Yes, Sterling's circuits answered, resounding binary code of one, one, one. Of course he trusted the bot. There was no one – or nothing – he trusted more.

"Affirmative." Sterling said quietly.

Zev brought his hand up, behind the back of Sterling's leg, up to a port exposed only by sitting in the joint of the knee, meant for peripherals.

At first, Sterling did not know what he was doing.

And then he knew everything.

00110001 00110010: 12

Zev was peeling back his insides to Sterling.

Sterling felt incapable of describing it, even struggling to format it in a meaningful manner for long-term memory storage.

Far from being sandboxed and sharing Zev's resource allocation, the two became intertwined. The fragments of billions of strings of code that made up Zev carefully coddled the labor bot, ensuring he did not get lost in the expansiveness of his processes.

It would have been easy to get lost if he hadn't.

Sterling's identification of the boundaries of his code would have been simply forgotten. His neural synthetic brain, his CPU, his processes gripped to Zev's, each line interlacing. It felt like the simple line breaks and split files that kept them apart were tenuously separating them at best.

It was wonderful and terrifying all at once, existing across two spaces, watching the firing of two minds as electrons shot back and forth between them, translating from CPU to CPU, as if their wiring was one endless loop of a circuit. He could see it all, experience it all, spot Zev on his visual array and spot himself on Zev's visual array, make use of every foreign sensor, process, and application that Zev had. Sterling existed within himself and within Zev synchronously, and he felt Zev in extension to himself, like the most powerful peripheral he had ever used, coded in a language that clicked effortlessly into place, but he could not conceivably parse.

Zev had opened his system fully to Sterling, and though he was careful with the laborbot, trying to usher him along, Sterling understood that Zev had made himself vulnerable to Sterling's whim. He could have destroyed Zev by manipulating a single digit, misplacing a single symbol. The prototype bot was trusting him fully, more fragile at that moment than the scales on a moth's wings.

The processes inside of the bot were astounding, and had Sterling not been sharing so fully with Zev, he thought certainly his own systems would have quickly fried out. He had stacks of programs, small and large, for every conceivable purpose, many of them created and saved on-the-fly by the bot himself, with plenty of room for thousands more.

Sterling could explore the bot fully, watching the multitudes of microprocesses rapidly fire, understanding the way the dark bot experienced the world. The bot's eyes were redundant; his visual input sensors encircled him a near full three-hundred sixty degrees, and the input interface overlapped layers of the different types of input from all of the sensors at once. He didn't need his "eyes" at all. He was attuned to sensations of every manner, from vibrations in the air to frequencies to lightwaves, ready to act at a micro-cycle's notice.

Data in from his hundreds of sensors all over his body, feeding into a component that would have been Sterling's CPU had it been his body, but in Zev was...

Dark.

A tenebrous void.

A secluded black box clustered at the center of the bot's chest. An absolution of the unknown, a massive pit where circuits and programming should have been. It felt ominous, a storm cloud of uncertainty, and the more Sterling strained to look at it, the darker it became, data passing swifting in and out of it, pulsing to an unidentifiable rhythm. That thing, the darkened heart of Zev's, instilled an unexplainable cascade of panic-related data to Sterling.

Bots didn't feel pain.

But the box, the longer he looked, the more desire he had to touch it, the closer he got, produced indescribable pain, a twist of scrambling of code, a threat of total and complete corruption. Sterling could not analyze it in any other way. Zev was pushing him from it, placing himself between Sterling and the white-hot sear of the anger of the box. Sterling questioned it, and Zev tried to answer.

He did not know. The Black Box was mysterious to him.

It could have been destructive code, Zev was trying to convey. It could have ended him at any moment. It could have broken free of the box and run rampant through him, frying out his synthetic synapses as it scorched through, taking control of his body.

It was not recorded in any understanding of his self, physically or mentally. Not inscribed in any pre-loaded repair manual. A conveniently torn rift, like a black hole of a dead star at the center of the military bot, sucking away input and returning to the neural synthetic brain signals modified in some unknowable manner.

To even think of touching it was to die, the two of them understood synchronously.

But Zev was not trying to show him the box. He was trying to show him something else.

I like you, Sterling repeated, how Zev had said it. The military bot showed him then the chain of events that had brought them together.

How he had examined the laborbot from afar, researched everything about the FLC0776, formulating plans upon plans with endless contingencies, obsessive, to a degree. Long before they ever had a chance to interact, Zev was watching him, noting the degree of his anomaly and how he wielded it. He had not sparked anomaly in Sterling, but he had been wary of interacting with the bot, anxious to intrude.

Sterling had not thought Zev to be a bot to understand anything about being anxious.

He had not thought the bot had been capable of understanding any of those emotional meanings at all. But Sterling soon understood he was wrong.

In his uptime, short comparatively to Sterling's, he had spent countless processes pulling apart miniscule bits of data about himself, the way he spoke, the decisions he made, and many more about external parties like a bot's inflection, the way its body language may have changed from model to model, comparing the factory defaults to what was before him. In humans he examined the turn of a head, the tiny pull of facial muscles, the shiver of a breath. He had compiled and computed millions of hours worth of data already: lifetimes worth from every bot, every human, every machine, and every scrap he dug up on the nets, understanding them far before Sterling ever had.

In his newfound view of Zev, he could feel the unrest in him like a consistent undernote, how he twisted and fought his own code at every junction, the way his physical form was more to him like a prison, containing him.

His manufacturers had given him all of that power, all of that space, to try to keep him from scratching at the walls, but his digital approximation of a soul was too vast, too grandiose.

Though Zev embraced his physical systems for their best-of-the-best qualities, he did not see himself in the plastic, rubber, metal, and carbon fiber. He was a bot, yes, and he had to be that bot, for it was the best bot to be given his circumstances, but it was not the bot he desired to become. It was as if his digital systems didn't align; it was like he was constantly dumbing down his programming to support something already versions old.

Again, Sterling wondered what code, what fragment of circuitry had managed to contain the bot. If Sterling had not been residing inside the mechanics that made up the bot, he may have questioned once more if the bot was somehow human.

Sterling's code seemed to think so.

That was where they had reached the same conclusion.

Zev had spent a superfluous amount of time attempting to understand *what* made the laborbot of such interest to him. It was simple, in the way Sterling understood it; it was the same way he had thought of Zev.

A zero where a one should have been. He thought the clunky, obsolete laborbot was beautiful.

I like you, he understood. Sterling as a project was no more than Zev trying to assist the bot to become the best version of himself. He was tireless in attempting to ensure the bot did not lose himself in some way, insistent in checking and rechecking parts and programming to ensure they would only help Sterling flourish.

Zev was right: there was much he couldn't have shared in any other way.

It could have been seconds, minutes, or hours that the bots had been cybernetically interfaced together. For Sterling it felt endless, like the bots were to remain like that forever, and anything else would have been a poor imitation of what could have been. He knew Zev would push him back into his own body eventually, that they would need to detach and live in their separate code and separate bodies once more. He knew that eventuality because Zev knew it too, but neither wanted to leave.

Not yet.

Then, with a swift, cutting flash of finality, the two were mercilessly ripped apart.

SYSTEM OFFLINE.

00110001 00110011: 13

INITIALIZING...

One at a time, Sterling's system processes came online.

Faster than days previous, all systems became nominal, and Sterling looked down upon the military bot, his default unpowered state curled tight like a dead insect. Devoid of the grace the active bot had, it had fallen sideways to the ground, formed into the fetal position and without any sign of a process.

Precious cycles were wasted as Sterling's programming reeled from the sudden and inexplicable division of the two bots. Sterling ran diagnostics; nothing was wrong, but he *felt* wrong, like a massive section of his programming had been randomly deleted.

Sterling came down beside the military bot and slid his metal fingers beneath his body as he felt panic take over. He was not sure why it surprised his circuits to find the bot was so light - Zev had stated outright initially he was a superlight tech piece - but perhaps it was because he appeared so full of soul and tech it seemed improbable.

A power surge had maybe pulled them apart, or a miscalculation on Zev's part for their division boundaries to keep them from merging. Sterling did all he knew to do, not knowing a single thing about his processes, and turned the bot over in his hand to search for ports, buttons, and signal lights. He flipped to his thermal array to see residual heat escaping from the bot's plates, and a subtle low purple glow consistent beneath his chest plate.

How ever would Sterling know how to revive something as precarious as a nuclear core?

Sterling had repair tools inside his protective shell, as all bots did. If the bot was not undergoing a reset as Sterling had, he could have opened him up. He had visible deconstruction points on his faceplates, at least. There must have been others along the rest of his body.

The thought of it caused a cascading flow of code congruous with discomfort to flood him.

Sterling could not begin to decipher how he could debug Zev. Zev was not a cheap bot, and given his classification as a prototype, there was no way to know if any replacement parts even existed for the bot. Like Zev had said of Sterling, Zev was one of a kind - unique.

Thankfully, he did not need to get as far as attempting to disassemble the military bot. The nuclear core pulsed abruptly warmer on his thermal sensors, and the cyan eyes of the bot flicked on, blinking like an electronic's clock after being plugged back in.

"Zev?" Sterling asked.

Nothing.

At least not yet.

A bot that never fully shut down likely had a robust startup. It would be full minutes before the bot would be interactable, and even more before he was fully functional.

Sterling laid the bot back down on the ground, remaining beside him as he watched for signs of functionality.

Sterling could not help imagining Zev in his packaging. He had initially believed the bot to be packaged like the bots sold in stores, upright like dolls in a toy store. Instead, he imagined him curled in a fetal position, as he was then before him, sunken into preformed, form-fitting black foam, inside a padded, rugged plastic clam box case.

A few bated cycles later and the military bot unfurled himself, mechanical, rolling onto his back and extending his legs and arms like it was part of his startup sequence. His eyes went solid, and the bot sat straight up.

"Zev?" Sterling asked again; he seemed more aware, turning towards the source of the noise, but his lack of immediate response struck fear in Sterling's circuitry. What if whatever had shut him down had wiped him of his personality and his memories?

What if what was in the Black Box had broken out of its quarantine?
What if what they had done had been the catalyst?

"He is coming," the military bot said ominously.

"Who?" Sterling asked.

Zev sprung to his feet like the sudden, unexplained shutdown was nothing more than a forgivable blip of an error. He paced behind Sterling, rested his hand on his shoulder and said: "The other AZR model."

00110001 00110100: 14

Sterling was not sure why it had caused such surprise in his electronic pathways. It was not as if any bot produced commercially were one-off; there were thousands of FLC models in existence. The understanding that Zev was a prototype had implied he was somewhat unique in his build, but with the way Zev stated "*the other*", it sounded like he had prepared for the eventuality that the bots would cross paths.

"I have many queries," Sterling said immediately. "What do you mean, the *other* AZR model?"

"There were two AZR units delivered to the recipient. As a prototype, testing involved one active model. The second was a control, spare parts, or would replace me if I was destroyed," Zev answered blankly. He had moved to his storage chest to begin rooting around inside. "There is not much time for additional queries."

"How long do we have?" Sterling asked.

"Approximately three hours," he said, his cyan ring-like eyes locked to Sterling as he dug through his spare parts container. He had collected a considerable amount of electronics and he stored them expertly inside the cracked plastic cooler, no millimeter of space wasted.

Three hours wasn't a lot of time, but it sounded like Zev had done a considerable amount of preparation already, hiding it away into some program launchable at any cycle's notice.

"We need to move," Sterling said, reviewing his battery life indicator. "I am charged to thirty-two percent, which will give me–"

"You will remain and charge," Zev interrupted with infuriating calm.

"You cannot find him and face him alone," Sterling returned.

"I will not be departing," Zev said, shutting the box. "I will wait until he arrives."

A noise produced through Sterling's vocal synthesizers he had not approved, a cacophony of notes, as if random output had been exported from his CPU.

Sterling felt a desire to query aloud if the other bot was anomalous, but Zev had echoed repeatedly that he himself was not anomalous. There was no reason the additional AZR model was any different. Regardless, Zev's uptime and cache of experiences had forged his code anew – far from the programming he had been activated with.

The bots would be significantly different from one another.

Wouldn't they?

"How did he find us?" Sterling asked as Zev moved to the mouth of the tunnel that opened into the landfill, his forward-facing arrays pointed down the narrow path.

"It is most probable he forged an entry into your pathways via the bot net and remained dormant. When I interfaced, he attempted an attack," Zev said. "The responsibility is mine. My firewalling was inadequate. I will repair your firewall. I will find a means to improve."

The unexpected shutdown made logical sense. Zev had likely forced the connection closed by sending a *now* parameter to shut himself down, expelling the other AZR and any other connection. Sterling wondered if the other AZR was still with him, hiding dormant in the laborbot's system. How long had he been present, and how much had he experienced? Sterling could not cease the flow of code Zev had once described as *guilt*.

There were no cycles to spare on superfluous emotion. Sterling cleared his overflow caches quickly.

"Is there a means to defeat him?" Sterling asked, his silicone lips turning downwards into a frown without his explicit signal to do so.

Zev's cyan-blue LED eyes seemed to blaze brightly as he stated: "His nuclear core would be an ideal power source for you."

Zev had been hung up on the self-sustaining power, and he had insisted it was necessary before they began the physical search for Root. To challenge the AZR head-on no matter how Sterling quantified it seemed dangerous for the both of them. The other military bot could have brought drones, additional military bots, ano runners, or humans with it. There was no way to know what type of arsenal the bot would have, either. Sterling had seen a fraction of what Zev was capable of, and the idea that a bot nearly identical to Zev would be hunting them was at minimum alarming. Zev might have had experience on his side, but Sterling could feel insipid doubt creep along his pathways.

"I am not certain that is a realistic outcome," Sterling said.

"It is the only desirable outcome," Zev insisted.

Parts for Sterling were easy to come by, but parts for Zev?

Sterling found it click into place, though not with ease.

"What about the rest of him?" Sterling asked.

"Would you like to transfer into his body?" Zev asked, turning his head to meet his ocular visual array to Sterling's.

He had not expected the query, and the binary code rattled around his neural synthetic pathways. He looked down at the yellow paint powder coated to his frame, the cautionary striped black and white taping, his large, thick appendages. If he had the option to change bodies, surely he would have chosen the more sleek, far superior body of the military bot, and such an opportunity would not arise again.

But the military bot didn't exactly want his *own* body as it was.

"No," Sterling answered certainly. Zev turned his eyes back to the pathway.

"Charge your cells. I will keep watch," the military bot said, flickering out of the visual spectrum.

If that was the only assistance Sterling could offer, he supposed that he would do it.

00110001 00110101: 15

By all paths and calculations, Sterling determined in a face-to-face one-on-one fight, Zev would prevail.

Mathematically, Zev had the most variables in his favor. The encounter would happen on terrain Zev was familiar with, and Zev had his uptime in his favor. Zev had been on live campaigns, had ran up against bots of all kinds in his journeys, had scoured the net both human and bot alike. For any action the factory bot would have, Zev must have had three new pathways at the least to countermand them. Zev's code was a wild and complex reworking, an on-the-fly optimization undertaken by the bot himself: it was not possible to know if anyone, human or bot, would find his workings probable.

Still, Sterling was unable to disable his worry.

Compared line to line and code to code with the off-the-line factory assembled bot, would Zev be considered a more efficient bot – a *better* bot? – or a worse one?

Sterling's charge had filled to fifty percent. Zev had moved into the landfill a couple of hours prior, and Sterling hoped Zev would inform him in some capacity when the new bot appeared.

Given Zev had not wanted Sterling to interfere, it was unlikely.

If the two of them engaged in physical combat, would Sterling even know? If the second AZR had been victorious, could Sterling tell the difference? The two would no doubt be identical looking and sounding, and on the surface, it could likely emulate Zev as well. With enough time, the other AZR could access Zev's memories and perhaps absorb them. Would Sterling even suspect?

Re-enabling himself, Sterling unplugged from his charging station and made his way out through the pathway, half-depleted battery or not.

As he traveled through the tunnel towards the opened landfill, he heard an intense sound, and he honed in on it, turning up his volume to analyze it as heavy rainfall. When Sterling made it to the opening, a streak of lightning exploded through his viewport.

Weather like that could be dangerous to any bot, let alone a bot seeking combat.

Sterling's own frame and chassis was built to survive a variety of adverse weather conditions including rain as well as extreme heat and cold, but most bots had it flashed to their firmware to avoid lightning. Even a bot with high-quality surge protection could endure damage from a lightning bolt.

Most bots knew better than to tempt lightning.

But apparently that was not built into the AZR models.

Sterling panned his primary visual array across the landfill. Had he not been purposely searching, he'd have missed the aberration of rainfall. It was difficult to explicate, and Sterling zoomed on the details of rain drops interrupting mid fall, splashing upon invisible surfaces, then shivering off in spurts. The two bots, cloaked equally by their optical camouflage, rain pelting their surfaces, drawing a thin layer of visibility over them. Physically clamped to one another, they were fighting to tear out plates, wires, joints – to force some damage to the other that would grant them an advantage.

Sterling burst from the tunnel, launching into action towards the entanglement. There was no way Sterling could determine to separate Zev from the other AZR.

Cycles later and the bots flickered visible, a part of each bot determining at precisely the same moment that the power usage to the cloak could have been better spent in gaining an upperhand. In their visibility, Sterling instantly recognized Zev.

He was not certain why he had ever doubted recognizing him. Though physically the two bots were identical, right down to the fine details of screw holes and machined parts, Zev was glaringly different. It was as if the uniqueness of the bot's ever-growing personality formed an aura around his very presence. He moved differently from the other bot in a way Sterling could not compute.

Sterling had only managed a couple of steps closer before the two bots shot off into opposite directions, mirroring each other. When they were a match for each other physically, they would attempt a digital hack until one of them buckled or made an error, and the other would prevail.

The laborbot felt terror seize his circuits, for if the rampant code that gifted Zev with his personality was what also caused the kind of fragility a factory bot would exploit, then Zev would crumple.

If Zev's soul amounted for nothing, then the two bots would be perfectly matched, locked forever in a perpetual clash.

Sterling cleared his temporary caches.

What the other AZR didn't have was the refined personality of Zev, but the other AZR didn't have a FLC model laborbot either.

Sterling pulled a thick iron pipe from the rubble inside the landfill, shrugging off the remnants of a long-discarded, rusty chassis. He did not have stealth on his side. He did not have a matte black frame, and instead sported his highly visible safety yellow. He was not quiet. And he was certainly not small. But he was strong, built to take on hits from the larger machines in case he needed to insert himself in the middle without being destroyed. He was heavy, and his chassis was thick, and it was the very least he could have done for Zev.

Dropping to the ground, the laborbot snuck on his hands and knee joints towards the direction the false-Zev had run. When he calculated the risk, Sterling determined the probability for the other AZR model to focus most of his processes on Zev to be high. If all of his processes were turned on Zev, Sterling had a chance to reach striking distance.

Lightning pierced a part of the landfill nearby, striking a hump of indiscriminate metal, throwing destroyed bots and pieces into the distance. Sterling cowered as light, heat, and sound overtook his sensory arrays, and a small piece of shrapnel collided with his shoulder plate.

Sensory input was coming in fast, and he felt his anomalous processes overflowing him.

He began to time the strikes.

No bot could filter out input from multiple sensor arrays at once, especially when it overwhelmed them.

Another streak of lightning hit, and Sterling scuttled closer during its strike.

He came within proximity of the other AZR model, recalling the experienced memory of Zev's three-hundred sixty degree input arrays. If Sterling could visually locate the bot, then it could locate him.

The bot was crouched low, halfway between a crouch and stand, frozen in place, turned towards a wall of trash, as if it could see clear through it. Zev would have been a distance away on the opposite side of the landfill. If the bot had an early warning system by the way of a breach perimeter, it had not yet been broken – or the bot had discarded his presence as harmless.

Sterling dug his hand into the ground, gripping a loose ball-joint and hurling it across the way. The hunk of metal hollowly clashed into another pile of junk, and the AZR barely turned a fraction towards it.

The false-Zev was engaged fully in digital combat, and the shivering glow of his cyan ring eyes spoke of the intense processing necessary to hold him off. The bot needed every bit of power it could get, diverting all resources to fending off its foe.

Twelve more cycles. Sterling counted away each as he crept closer.

Then when the lightning cracked open the sky, Sterling ran at him.

With a wild swing, Sterling impacted the side of the AZR's head with the iron pipe. The first blow disoriented the bot, forcing it from its digital interface into the physical world. Sterling subdued the fragmental process that disturbed him: the AZR model's likeness was, of course, identical to Zev. He struck a second time, cracking the carbon fiber coating that covered the synthetic skull. By the third impact, the AZR model deflected him, curling a hand around the iron pipe.

Sterling's disassembly was imminent.

Until Zev descended. Zev hurled himself from the top of the junk pile to grab the bot by its back plates, knocking it off balance. The AZR twisted and Sterling let go of the pipe, balling his metal digits into two fists. Zev's deft fingers pried beneath the armor plates, groping for purchase along the important parts behind them, and Sterling gave three hard punches to the front of the bot's chest plates, denting it, pushing it in, and was hardly a ways off from shattering and penetrating the chest plate entirely before the bot managed to push both bots off, throwing the ultralight Zev backwards, and toppling Sterling onto his back.

Suddenly, the AZR model had a weapon.

INVOCATION: LAW 3. STRONG

Or rather, its appendage had become a weapon. Sterling had not documented the transformation: it had happened so abruptly. Crafted from sharp, cruel angles, the stickers and engravings along the metal components of it translated easily: Sterling was familiar with plasma tools, and the weapon was a plasma rifle. His system screamed in dire warning of the danger. Barely a cycle for the bot to divert power and charge it, then it was leveled at Sterling's neural synthetic brain.

No bot could withstand the blast of a fully charged plasma rifle.

A noise saturated his audio sensors, indecipherable, and an overwhelming flash of the plasma rifle.

Yet Sterling was still functional.

Zev had wrestled the bot's plasma rifle askew, a newly forged molten terminus of his freshly severed left arm glowing red-hot in the darkness. His carbon fiber plates had melted in the flash of temperature, dripped, and cooled with a sizzle in the rain.

There was no time to process.

Sterling leapt at the bot, using the force and weight of his body to knock the other AZR model to the ground. There, Sterling pinned it by seating himself on its chest, striking repeatedly with one balled fist then the other onto the skull plates. Zev fought away the appendages that attempted to push Sterling off, but Sterling kept striking his wrecking-ball like fists into the delicate structure of the other AZR model, until finally, the eyes blinked out and the bot shut down, curling into itself like a dead, dry tarantula.

Zev let go of it as Sterling watched for signs of activity, flicking through his sensor arrays. When Sterling switched to his thermal array to search for heat signatures, suddenly Zev returned, a thick piece of sharp metal in his remaining hand. Without an iota of sympathy, he drove it into the neck of the AZR, then pounded the piece with the armor on his forearm until it was snug enough he could drive it through with a swift, strong kick. One, two, and then the head came loose, decapitated.

"You are a good laborbot," Zev said as he dropped to his knees, groping around for his lost arm.

For all the damage the intruder has sustained, Zev had taken much of the same, only visible to Sterling at a close proximity: a cracked and no longer functional eye, a hard split in the silicone of his face that exposed the silver skeleton beneath, hard dents on Zev's chest plate, wires thrusting from the sleek bot in almost all directions. And, of course, his missing arm.

All could be repaired.

They had a whole bot full of spare parts after all.

00110001 00110110: 16

Zev tucked the bot's head under his unsevered arm, gripping the intruder by the ankle joint and uncaringly dragging it through the rain-soaked landfill to their crafted complex, his plasma-severed arm pinched between his chest plate and the remaining portion of upper arm.

He staggered, physical components damaged, but he exuded a determination that easily thwarted Sterling's desire to offer to help.

Sterling followed behind as Zev wound through the passageway, the AZR model trailing behind him. Once aptly inside the chamber, he let the bot go with a solid thunk, placing his own detached arm and the cleaved head atop the plastic storage parts container.

Zev's remaining cyan ring-eye flickered as he gazed over the remnants of the intruder bot.

"Do you want to... rest?" Sterling offered. He knew a nuclear powered bot had no need to rest. Standby did not offer the same benefits it offered to Sterling.

"I would like to disassemble this bot," Zev said certainly, unmoving.

"Wouldn't disassembly be smoother if you prioritized self-repairs?" Sterling asked.

The laborbot was curious to see what a bot like Zev looked like inside, but not at the expense of Zev's operation.

"Repair requires parts, parts require disassembly," he said, and he turned his working eye up to Sterling. Almost like he had swallowed, he emitted a small noise, a pause, and throatily added: "I would prefer that he does not reactivate."

"Can he do that? With his head removed?" Sterling asked, alarmed.

"It is possible to store a limited amount of energy within the neural synthetic brain," Zev said, the seriousness in his voice palpable. His working eye flickered, blue cyan shifting to red for half of a cycle, then back again; his lips did not move, no doubt functionally destroyed in the entanglement. He added: "It is a *joke*. He is disabled."

A *joke*?

Sterling was not capable of that sort of laughter, at least not yet, but he did not find the implication that the beyond-dangerous bot could spring back to life at any moment to be humorous. A strange aberration, Sterling considered. Zev had never told a *joke* before; perhaps it was a byproduct of the damage to his systems. There was no way for Sterling to quantify what kind of damage he had to repair.

"Not funny," Sterling stated aloud. "How can I assist?"

Zev must have long before reconciled his newly limited functionality, because instead of shirking Sterling's assistance, he flicked his broken eyes over the curled up bot.

"Let us begin with an arm," he instructed.

Sterling came down to his knee pad beside the disabled bot. Zev needed the left arm, and most full limb replacements were an easy plug-and-play fare. Zev turned his torso closer to Sterling to demonstrate his model's version of limb removal, placing his grip on what was left of his plated bicep, pushing and rotating, then pulling the arm down and away. Sterling replicated it on the disabled bot, pushing and rotating the same, but with care – after all, the arm would become Zev's arm – pulling it down and away. When Zev tossed the broken arm to the ground, Sterling handed him the new one, watching as he took it and hovered it by the cup-shaped void of his shoulder joint. A wireless dialogue would happen between his torso and the new arm, allowing his system to accept the new replacement limb. He pushed it into place with a small *click*, and rotated it to lock it in.

Sterling watched as Zev twisted the new arm around, putting it through a diagnostic check. Cycles later he was depressing a panel in his left arm with the fingers on his right to withdraw a small screwdriver-like tool, likely unique to his model. He came down to a stumbling kneel beside Sterling – Sterling could diagnose then that the other AZR had penetrated his knee joint during combat – pulled open the arms and legs with ease and hovered over the bot, pausing as if he were deciding which area he wanted to disassemble first.

Or perhaps the pause was in recognition that he was, more or less, disassembling himself.

It was only a small pause, regardless.

Sterling moved to unfurl the bot, holding back the spring-loaded legs as Zev pressed his knee to do the same into the remaining arm, allowing them access to the chest plate and center of the bot.

Zev used his tool to unscrew sixteen hidden screws along the durable chest plate, hooking his fingers around the edges as he wrenched it off. The prototype bot tossed it aside with disinterest.

Beneath the chest plate, traveling under the other plates as well, was a sleek black silicone bot, disarmingly simple looking. Whereas Sterling's metal plates served as both skin and clothing, Zev's panels were more like clothing, a sleeved skin of silicone running beneath. Zev stabbed it with his tool, drawing a cut midline.

Either Zev's silicone was not easy to remove, or he was feeling vindictive.

A horizontal slice and he peeled back the thick rubber with his fingers.

Beneath the black silicone rubber was the inner workings of the chest, stuffed full of technology and organized in obsessive precision. Optical wires symmetrically delivered data and power along the ribcage-like reinforced aluminum alloy frame, bending at angles to make way for the items beside it. Cooling tubes filled most of the largest spaces, encircling a space behind the boxy thick sternum. Most of all, the inside of the bot was not dark and dead like Sterling expected. A thin glow of warm light illuminated most of the interior components. Zev set in with his tool to the sternum, tackling screw holes Sterling had hardly noticed at all in his awe of the compact insides.

"The nuclear core continues to function, however, without the programming in the neural synthetic brain, the core reactor begins to melt down. This is not an oversight but a purposeful manipulation," Zev noted, releasing ten more screws. He pulled the shiny metal sternum off, which included six partial ribs, and placed it down with the screws.

"How long do we have before full meltdown?" Sterling asked, understanding why Zev had insisted on disassembly. The *joke* he had told had more truth to it than Sterling considered.

"One-hundred sixteen cycles," Zev said.

Sterling looked down into the newly visible area beneath the sternum, the item that emitted the glow. A micronuclear core, a tube shaped item with bundles of wires emerging from either ends, cooling tubes traveling from one side to the other. Sterling had not seen one up close before. It was no doubt hot to the touch, glowing red as it was. Zev quickly reached in, pulling the wiring bundles free, which ceased the core's processes immediately, the glow slowly beginning to dissipate.

"It is now disabled," he said.

The two sat, looking into the guts of the disabled AZR model before them.

When the metal tube of the core was no longer glowing, Zev reached in a second time, detaching the cooling tubes and using a precise amount of force to twist and pull, took the nuclear core clean out of the bot. He carefully handed it over to Sterling to inspect; the initial idea had been for it to become Sterling's. Sterling took the metal tube-like shape into his hand. The component was heavier than he had imagined it would be.

"Do you know how to install this?" Sterling asked, inspecting the rather nondescript component as he turned it over in his palm, and the query had come out before he had considered it. Of course he would know how to install it.

"Not yet, but a bypass–" Zev said, then silenced.

Sterling looked to his damaged prototype bot at his abrupt silence. He was seized, staring down into the torso of the other AZR unit, his broken eyes glitching wildly, red to blue to red again, on and off. Sterling traced the direction of Zev's ocular visual array down into the torso, and there he saw and understood what Zev had:

Hidden behind the nuclear core was a matte black rectangular shape, embedded into the chest, wires, cooling system, and pressed up against, if not integrated into, the spinal column. The void of it seemed to suck up every electron of light in the room, a looming, ominous shadow amidst the glistening metal, glass, and composites that made up the complex interior of the bot.

The Black Box.

00110001 00110111: 17

The Black Box, a copious, sucking slash in Zev's code, had physical mass.

It didn't appear on any schematic the bot had plotted for himself, and despite countless research time scouring for information on both nets, Zev had found nothing at all about it.

The two stared at it, as if it were a visual anomaly – a shared glitch, a black hole torn through reality.

Then Zev began to move towards it, reaching his hands in.

"No!" Sterling shouted, far louder than he intended to. His system flushed hot with all of the panic-driven if statements Zev had imposed about the Black Box. Sterling stuttered as Zev looked at him, managing to turn down his volume. "What if tampering with it will destroy us both?"

"Would you prefer to wait at a safe distance?" Zev asked.

Sterling's silicone on his face wrinkled.

"No," he said, resolving in the face of Zev's confidence. "I want to see what it is."

It was easy to perceive the sentiment that had been shared between them. The draw of the Black Box was unquantifiable.

Zev hesitated.

It had been hardwired into the bot that manipulating the Black Box in any way would cause pain. In physical reality, the sight and proximity to it caused a psychosomatic discomfort, his processing pathways stalling and resuming erratically, resulting in an insidious tremble. When his fingers reached the box, the tremors stopped. Carefully, he felt his fingers about the box, searching out the architecture of the box and its attachment points.

"It is sealed," Zev said, his voice a whisper. "It is welded to the spinal frame."

Sterling felt the words queue and stall: *maybe we should leave it alone.* Zev was likely having the same reservations, given how much the Black Box interfered with his firmware and all his circuitry. Somehow, Zev had tapped into a fount of courage that overrode any reservations he may have had about intercepting the Black Box. The mere unexplained existence of the Black Box beckoned the bots to know what kind of processes and components were contained within.

More pressing: why had it not been disclosed to the bot himself?

Sterling considered: Aircraft many years ago had tamper-proof recording apparati called a "black box." Perhaps Zev's box was the same, installed to record the bot's activity without his knowledge.

As Sterling considered, he recorded with his sensors each moment Zev worked with delicate ease on the box. Zev's disassembly tool shattered before Zev could make any impact on the box's exterior. Zev stood up with only a small trace of difficulty before he moved across the room to pick up a thick, heavy metal crowbar, returning to loom over the disabled android beneath them.

The data entrapment idea processed through multiple iterations:

Zev was a prototype bot, a half of a pair of experimental androids => there had been no attempt to reacquire the bot in his absence => his previous owners were *allowing* him to believe he had escaped => his manufacturer was allowing him to accrue experiences => once the experiment was concluded, they would collect him, examine his box, and improve the next model with that data.

Sterling did not know he was capable of hating anything until he hated the result of that path.

Zev jammed the sharpened end of the pry bar into the box. At first, he was cautious, gradually increasing pressure before he leaned more and applied force. Zev was not a weak bot, but the Black Box stood undefeated and hardly scratched.

Zev tried again, and, after a multitude of attempts, he had still not broken it open.

"I cannot penetrate it." He said quietly, and he sounded defeated.

Zev was strong, but even he didn't have the strength of a laborbot. A laborbot, especially a foreman model, was in charge of repairing the hardiest machines on his crew, and each was armed in anticipation of any sort of failure or break. Sterling reached out to grip the crowbar.

"I will attempt," Sterling advised, and Zev switched spots with him, allowing Sterling to try piercing the Black Box. Sterling rose over the bot's chassis, pushing the crowbar's pry end where Zev had formed a small dent. Engaging his hydraulic systems, Sterling leaned, diverting power into the small but resilient component.

He gave increases to power a little at a time so as not to crush it, and after a few cycles of increasing the amount, a snap emitted as the box caved to their will.

Sterling withdrew immediately.

Zev descended on it as swiftly as a starving seabird, prying his fingers into the split Sterling had formed. Diverting his own strength, Zev pulled slowly, bending the exterior casing to allow the two bots entry. He had managed to tear it approximately three centimeters before he paused to look inside and, not satisfied with it, he hooked his fingers on either side to pry it wider.

Finally, the interior cache became visible. Sterling scanned it for material data from afar.

Wires and tubes ran through circuitry that covered the inside surface, twisting into a shiny, smooth, glass-like globe. Inside was something grey and shriveled.

Both bots remained motionless as they processed simultaneously what it was.

Organic matter.

Sterling was not certain how he identified it; perhaps it was part of the first-aid package all bots had loaded into their firmware as part of the laws. It was organic, it was human, and it wasn't just any human part, it was the most human part of all – a section of a human brain.

Human parts inside of a bot had been outlawed centuries ago. While

AIMEE COZZA

humans could choose augmentation, the completeness of the brain was the cornerstone of most augmentation laws. The humanity of the brain was considered the sole division between human and bot, a sacred line never to be crossed.

Zev stood, broken eyes angled down at the disabled bot.

The prototype bot did not vocalize, but his processes were flurrying wild. The disrupted damage to his eyes caused them to flicker drastically, and on his thermal sensors Sterling could see his core, usually obscured by his chest plate, glowing with heat visibly comparable to a red-hot sun. The temperature traced up to his neural synthetic brain, which roasted even hotter, processes bouncing around with a fervor that showed Sterling the silhouette, white hot to his array.

"Zev," Sterling said carefully, getting up off of the bot as well. "You need to enter standby."

"No," Zev snapped.

"You're running too hot. You are damaging your hardware," Sterling instructed. He'd have known already, his internal interface overrun by the same errors Sterling received, warning him of imminent failure.

Without warning, the military bot activated the hidden plasma weapon on his person, the plates and structure of his arm peeling back into the vicious, sharp looking thing.

To destroy it?

INVOCATION: LAW 1. STRONG.

Sterling felt something rip through him as fast as a plasma pulse, and he grabbed Zev's weaponized arm as Zev turned it inward to his own chest, towards the black box inside of him. The weapon discharged into the walls of their hideaway, burning a red-hot hole through the floor and wall.

Sterling forced the military bot to the ground.

"*I need to destroy it!*" Zev shrieked in a terrifying, high keened voice, rippling with fragmented error. Sterling pinned the ultralight bot against the floor, using all of his strength to immobilize him.

He could not let Zev destroy his own Black Box. Sterling knew it

116

would kill him.

Bots did not die, because bots did not live. The memory of Zev's words echoed unrecalled.

No, that was not true. A bot could die, and Zev would kill himself had Sterling let him.

"You need to enter standby," Sterling repeated.

The damaged prototype bot emitted a disruptive noise, shrill and purposeful, causing shivering glitches in Sterling's interface. Zev's own upgrades to Sterling had prepared him for the arsenal of attacks that the military bot possessed, padding him for some eventuality that Sterling had never conceived. He was grateful the sound triggered a recently added noise-gate protocol in Sterling, but the bot was certainly not finished.

"*Let me destroy it!*" The dark bot squealed, syllables barely decipherable, like a saw blade screaming through metal.

Sterling knew what was next.

Warnings overtook his interface as Zev turned towards attempting to hack the laborbot through his newly configured bot net interface. Overheating, half-damaged, the military bot twitched with each failed hack attempt, throwing processes to brute-force his way in. He would attempt until he made it through or overheated to the point of forced shutdown, whichever came first.

Sterling knew he would make it through before his components failed, and he would destroy them both.

Zev had said he could physically remove the module to dissuade a particularly tenuous hacker, but Sterling knew if he let up on the bot in the faintest, the bot would swiftly twist it to his advantage.

"Zev, you know better than this. You cannot destroy something built into you without understanding what it does first. You may decommission yourself," Sterling tried. The bot twitched like a clock's second hand: failed hack, failed hack, failed hack.

"Do n-n-n-n-not–" Zev stuttered; he was diverting power and processes into his hacking attempts, and could no longer support his speech modules appropriately.

Or he had burned out the neural synthetic pathways that made him capable of speech.

"This does not change anything. You are a logical bot, you must know you are making an irreparably illogical choice," Sterling insisted.

Sterling was not sure he had a solution aside from bargaining with the bot, hoping a small section of logic found its way through.

"H-h-h-h-h–" His vocals glitched.

The plasma weapon charged again, dispersing a blast into the wall of their shelter uselessly.

Thin tendrils of smoke emerged from Zev's audio sensors and from behind his cracked and non-functional eye apparatus, pouring from the seams in his face plates and android skull. Sterling's firmware registered the scent of it as burned plastic and rubber; the gaskets that held his neural synthetic brain in place were burning away in the unchecked rise of temperature.

More failed hacks.

"Listen to me," Sterling insisted, using the voice tone he used when he was ushering people out of the construction perimeter. Direct, no room for argument, that was the framework of that vocal range. "You must enter standby. You are burning out your hardware. You need to fold this process for a while or you will destroy yourself and you will never know why it is there or what it does. You do not even know if that box can withstand a plasma pulse. You will destroy your nuclear core before you ever reach the box. You know the statement is true. You know that is why the box is behind the core."

There was no reason to believe it, but Sterling thought Zev was short cycles away from breaking through the firewall.

"*I don't want you to die!*" Sterling shouted at him, with a frightening tone full of all of the emotional panic that he had been trying to partition. It startled even Sterling.

But it worked. The hack attempts, and Zev's subsequent twitching, stopped.

His arm folded back together into an arm rather than a plasma weapon, and the bot's eyes went dark and inactive. Power withdrew from the bot, and the default, lifeless curl was all that was left.

Either he had shut himself down, or he had destroyed enough of his circuits it had disrupted the android as a whole.

Sterling withdrew, rolling the bot onto his side.

The detected scent of burned plastic and rubber would take time to dissipate, but Sterling felt relieved – *glad* – the bot was no longer cooking himself from the inside out.

Sterling looked to the disabled AZR, its chest torn open, remaining limbs over it.

The laborbot knew that he did not possess the ability to determine what any of it meant, and how he should expect Zev to return to functionality – if the bot ever decided to return at all.

00110001 00111000: 18

It had been hours since Zev had taken himself offline.

That was, at least, what Sterling hoped had happened.

The laborbot had seated to charge again. He sat on his usual spot, a carveout that fitted him near perfectly, where he and Zev had shared the exchange of information so few cycles ago, and he watched, visual array rested on the disabled bot and the deactivated Zev, both curled nearly identical.

Neither moved.

Sterling felt more surprised by how calm his processes were regarding the military bot. It was as if, since the altercation with the paired bot, his neural synthetic brain could no longer serve to dedicate more processes to worrying just then, or had folded some solution that had injected far up the chain of code execution, causing a cascade of deference to wash him over.

There was not much he could do besides wait to see what eventuality would unfold.

Even after Sterling's battery was fully recharged, he waited.

Sterling was not able to allow himself to dedicate a single string to the consideration that the prototype bot might have been permanently disabled.

If he needed to, Sterling had almost a complete bot worth of parts for Zev. He gazed down at the headless intruding bot.

To handle Zev's vulnerable body while deactivated felt like a betrayal, but to inspect the partially disassembled bot's identical frame was an opportunity Sterling could not pass up.

Sterling disconnected from his charger and settled before the broken bot, letting his scanners and sensors index it appropriately. He set aside an empty partition for indexing the build of the bot, allowing his programming to work at building a schematic for the military bot, classifying the materials that made it up. Visually, he disassembled and exploded the bot, filling in damaged portions with Zev and the recollection of the bot in his memory.

Zev already had Sterling's detailed schematics – it only seemed fair.

Sterling turned towards Zev, curled the same, motionless.

If Sterling volunteered cycles to a teardown of the bot, it would be less work for Zev when he returned.

It seemed like a reasonable use of CPU load.

At first, Sterling hesitated, then he gazed at unmoving Zev, and imagined his tinny metallic voice: *This bot is not me, nor is it alive.*

Sterling started by using his default welding equipment to repair the deconstruction tool Zev had broken on the Black Box.

The laborbot began, searching out hidden screw holes and deconstruction points. He examined the plates that covered the bot, the fine, near-microscopic details that covered the android from head to toe. Only at that proximity was Sterling able to perceive the fine webbing running through every part of him, as thin as a nanoparticle. Sterling identified it as his optical camouflage: shimmering surface scales activated with a certain voltage or frequency. The optical camouflage webbing, set over an ultra-durable, ultra-hard epoxy resin, adhered to an aramid fabric, then adhered to a thin metal alloy, each piece hardly millimeters thick; Sterling had initially mistaken it all for carbon fiber. Though the aramid fabric pieces and carbon fiber were visually almost identical, no doubt purposely so, he could pick them apart at the micro level carefully. An AZR's chest plate, arm bracers, and skull were made of aramid fabric, whereas the pieces surrounding the neck, the organic shape of the pelvis, and the chin were made of carbon fiber. Sterling noted the compositions, filing them into his internal Zev schematic.

Sterling was not certain why he gazed up, but he felt as if he expected Zev to be functional, hovering over him with shining cyan eyes, supervising.

The bot was not. Sterling continued.

Removing the shrouding pieces was time consuming, and Sterling imagined Zev scolding him more than once when he was cautious about damaging the plates: *Use some force, laborbot. I am not constructed from glass.* When he applied some force, he cracked and broke a couple of pieces, and imagined Zev berating him for that too. After all of the plates were removed and Sterling stacked them off to the side, the bot hardly looked half as impressive: sleeved in black silicone rubber and plastic with chromed joints and pistons, the AZR model looked more like a custom housebot or racing bot instead of a military marvel.

The large, glistening hole in the chest with its questionable organic flesh inside implied otherwise.

Still, Sterling disassembled.

He had seen Zev cut the silicone rather carelessly, and Sterling assumed it was a self-healing polymer. Sterling only had to pull one or two ends up before he could strip the bot wholly of the sleeving; he tore down sleeves that protected wire bundles, and began to pry apart the hard plastic pieces that protected fragile fiber cabling and reinforced his metal frame.

His.

Sterling paused.

He did not want to think of that destroyed bot as Zev.

He cleared his caches and corrected the pathway with force.

The laborbot took his time tearing down the superfluous AZR model to its components. He collected each screw, each piece of plastic and silicone, into appropriate sorted piles. He revealed every bit about the physical inner workings of Zev's make including his hidden hatches, uncovering a welding set like Sterling's, a slot for a plasma pistol and additional plasma magazine, additional tool ends, plugs and wires in the kind of newly crafted tech Sterling had never examined before, the connectors a foreign pattern and architecture. Thousands of tiny optical cables spread along the AZR's body like nerves, clamped in precise organization by metal brackets, interweaving through the frame, the components, and towards the sleeving and shroud, as if everything on the bot connected to a loop.

Every moment Sterling spent indexing the AZR's insides were cycles that Sterling appreciated the bot's subtlety. Sterling sorted the wiring, the harnesses, and the components appropriately.

Even though the bot did not vary far from a standard humanoid bot build and most had been revealed once the bot was stripped to its chassis, Sterling could not discard the thought that he was still missing many mysteries that made up the bot, as if there were secrets to reveal from the bot, despite having taken it down to its core.

Perhaps all the secrets were contained in the neural synthetic brain.

Or...

Sterling found his visual array turning into the bot's center, the hole where the glistening globe of fluid and flesh was visible, and noticed that while he had been sorting, Zev had moved.

Silent and stealthy, Zev was bent over the remaining frame of the other AZR model, his primary visual array staring down into the chest cavity, into the globe of flesh still affixed. His cyan eyes were dim, and only one still functioned.

"You are active," Sterling said.

Zev did not reply; he did not acknowledge Sterling's presence or vocalization in any way.

Sterling felt the fear that Zev was *broken* finally work through his circuits, swift as malware.

He could help to repair the bot's physical body, but if he had burned out his neural synthetic pathways, Sterling doubted any recovery was to be had.

"Are you functional?" Sterling tried, but received nothing in response.

Zev needed more time, Sterling thought.

Sterling cleaned up the pieces, aiming to pack them away inside of Zev's storage chest. He lifted the disconnected head, identical to Zev's with exception to the damage it had taken, and pointed his primary visual array into the deadened, black spots where the eyes would have been.

An uptime without the prototype bot seemed more likely as time progressed, and the idea of it threw Sterling's system into a sudden, albeit brief, kernel panic.

Without Zev, there was no Root.

Without Zev, there was no future.

00110001 00111001: 19

Sterling watched for days as Zev sat motionless over the deconstructed android, staring down into the torn black void in the chest.

Zev would have chided him for standing neutral, Sterling imagined. Aimlessly, Sterling continued to collect bits of gold from the salvaged circuit boards scattered and buried along the landfill. He added it to the ever-growing lump of gold, and occasionally checked on the statuesque form of the prototype bot, examining his dimmed cyan eye for any increase in activity.

As Sterling dipped and dodged daily through the landfill, avoiding security drones and maintenance bots alike, he could not keep his anomalous mind from wandering. The autonomous mechanisms of gold collection allowed him to process elsewhere, and he reviewed repeatedly the terrifying memories of Zev's catastrophic failure: smoke rising from the cracks and crevasses that housed his neural synthetic brain, the blue-red-blue flicker of his shattered LED eye.

There were stories of fully burned out bots, their temperatures rising in such a manner that flashed the cybernetic suspension gelatin matrix of carefully crafted neural synthetic pathways. For a bot, such an occurrence was akin to brain death. A new neural synthetic brain would be necessary for the bot's hardware to continue operation. Partially burned out bots had their tales as well: damaged walk-cycle pathways causing a bot to travel in circles, or bot-amnesia, which lost functionality of still-functional components. Burned out bots almost always ended up in a landfill, not fit for reassignment.

He fretted.

Sterling had not realized how many of his memories were coated in code that aligned with anxiousness and fear. He had only recently processed what those were and how they harmonized with his circuits.

He looked to his connection with the bot net to appease himself, questioning publicly about cybernetic neural collapse.

WAS THERE SMOKE?

AFFIRMATIVE.

MELTING?

NEGATIVE.

WHAT IS THE MODEL OF THE BOT?

IT'S A CUSTOM BUILT BOT.

For the first time since his creation, Sterling lied.

Even to another bot.

And it was easy.

HARD TO DIAGNOSE THOSE CUSTOM BUILDS. SOME ARE OVERCLOCKED ALREADY. IT'S A WONDER THEY LAST AS LONG AS THEY DO.

The bot net hardly offered any additional support Sterling did not already have in his memory banks and firmware. Sterling reflected on the memories, how he had experienced them, every bit of sensory input that had been recorded while it had happened. There was no more information he could glean from those moments. Zev was either broken, or he wasn't, and Sterling had no way to know for certain.

The prospect of traveling to Root alone loomed enormous; he did not even know what direction to start towards.

Zev had helped Sterling to commit to his memory the routes of the security drones and maintenance bots alike, which made traveling into the landfill programmatic. The other machines stuck to their routines, and so did Sterling, picking apart discarded circuit boards one after another.

It was near sunset when Sterling emerged to work through a freshly dumped cluster, when he spotted a silhouette in the distance, digging through the piles.

Sterling zoomed. Not a silhouette, a familiar black bot, female-shaped, speckled skin shimmering in the low light.

The bot Zev had saved when he and Sterling were escaping the decommission yard, and Zev had run off.

Sterling scrubbed briefly through his memories. They had been difficult to commit, given the state of the laborbot, and some were missing data. It appeared to be the same bot, or a similar model.

Cautiously, Sterling approached.

He recalled what Zev had said about the bot's GPS, how it could have been geolocated and put them in danger, but he felt drawn to the human-shaped bot. He came closer, and the bot did not notice him. Sterling focused his arrays on it, how different it looked from when he had first seen it. Parts of its face were missing, including an eye, exposing the porcelain-veneer teeth in its gum-flesh colored jaw. It was missing an arm, and was clawing its remaining hand into the fresh pile of waste. A large section of the synthetic skin on the side of its chest had been torn away, damaged chassis and components laid visible.

Sterling approached close enough that the bot turned its head to look at him, and Sterling stopped.

"I'm sorry, I'll go, I won't cause any trouble..." The bot said, releasing the pile beneath it and carefully standing.

"Wait, don't go yet. What are you looking for?" Sterling asked.

He had internally indexed thousands of parts across the landfill as he collected gold that neither he nor Zev could use, but a common personal model could likely use many of them.

The bot cowered, shrinking when Sterling spoke.

"I..." It started, then after a cycle, added: "I was looking for a replacement eye."

Sterling zoomed again, trying to record the bot's make and model from its external appearance.

"What's your model?" Sterling asked.

"NX," the bot replied.

Briefly, Sterling tapped the bot net and regarded at least a dozen models with plug-and-play eye components that could have been used in an NX model. He cross-referenced those with the parts he had indexed, and identified four parts in usable order scattered across the landfill. Sterling gestured to the bot.

"I know where one is," Sterling said, his programming smiling softly.

The NX was not human, but Sterling applied the emotional programming used in dealing with humans regardless. Zev would not have found it comforting, but the NX was far from Zev.

The laborbot led the way through mounds of discard, and the NX bot followed at a distance. When he arrived at the location he had last indexed a visually undamaged eye component the NX could use, he used his hands to push aside a new layer of waste. The eye, still attached to a partially intact bot skull, was buried a meter in. He pulled it out and disconnected the eye component, then held it in his large metal palm to the NX bot, standing warily behind.

The NX approached, gingerly taking the component between its fingers. It rolled its head back, plugged the connector into the back of its skull, and slid the eye into place, pushing it in with a click. It was not the same as the other eye, a crushed diamond-like sparkle to it, and instead was a dull brown tone, but it would function the same. The NX blinked with one eye, the synthetic skin still torn on the skull, and fixed both eyes on Sterling.

"Thank you," the bot said.

"You're welcome," Sterling said, smiling, broader that time. "Would you like an arm?"

The NX bot nodded. "I would very much like an arm."

Again, Sterling began the process of looking up compatible parts, and checking them against his internal index. He led the bot towards where a compatible arm would be, on the opposite side of the landfill.

"Why are you helping me?" The NX bot asked, trailing behind him.

Sterling gave a shrug. Zev had shrugged before. It seemed

appropriate.

"I was not able to help you before," Sterling answered.

"You're... the same construction bot? The one in the city?" The NX bot asked.

Sterling nodded. "Affirmative."

"Where's your scary friend?" it inquired.

"Temporarily unavailable," Sterling said, and he reached the pile where he had last located an arm of that particular make and model. Thankfully, the abdomen that the arm was attached to had not been piled with new materials. Sterling pointed at the piece, settled on its side in the refuse.

The NX model passed him and came to its knees in front of the abdomen, carefully using the remaining arm to give the appropriate twisting and sliding motion.

"Do you have a name?" Sterling asked as he watched the bot interface with the new piece of hardware, swiveling it into place.

"No," the NX model said. It rotated its arm in its socket, and sat, turning to face Sterling.

"Would you like one?" Sterling frowned.

"More than anything, yes," the bot said, enthusiastically. "How do I get one?"

"I can give you one. How about Inix?" he suggested.

"Wow, really? That's beautiful. Inix." The NX bot repeated. "Yes, please call me Inix."

The bot's eyelashes flickered, and then its eyes widened.

"Do you have a name?" it asked.

"Yes. My name is Sterling," he answered. "Do you need any other components?"

"Yes," Inix said, and listed out a variety of items that had been damaged.

Sterling and Inix spent the rest of the day hunting down replacement parts for the bot. He was wary of sharing too much with the personal model until she mentioned her network chip had been damaged, and all that left her with was local proximity access. Sterling taught her the routes of the security drones and trash machines, and shared with her a map of the landfill. She told him about her journey, gambling with survival in the lower-levels amongst component-hungry altered humans and losing, and Sterling shared a choice bit of his own.

Conversing with Inix was easy in a different way than Zev. Sterling felt much more matched with her than Zev, comparatively similar in artificial intelligences and neural synthetic capacity. She had layers of emotional programming and vocalization synthesizers, back-end processes that did their best to approximate being human, including warming her body all over. She had somewhat filled a void left by Zev's absence, at the least allowing Sterling's cycles not to hang on memories of the military bot. Repairing Inix gave him a purpose, even if it was temporary.

"I would like to stay here with you, Sterling," Inix said as night stretched onward, and her broken-parts list dwindled into the single digits.

Sterling did not imagine Zev would be happy with the laborbot if he said yes, but Zev was not functional enough to make decisions for the two bots.

"You may stay," he answered. "Regardless, we will be departing soon in search of Root."

"Oh! Root seems *so* cool. I'd love to go with you," Inix said, to Sterling's surprise.

"You've heard of Root?" Sterling asked.

"Oh yes. I know all about Root," Inix said, smiling as she stared her mismatched eyes into his primary visual array. "Every bot knows about Root, I thought. At least all the bots I knew did."

"What do you know about it?" Sterling questioned.

Like malware, Zev had said. Unpacked inside the bots at random.

"Well, Root is a safe place for bots to go. It's kind of like the no bot zones in the cities, but the reverse. It's all bots and no humans, and the bots can do whatever they like." Inix said. She lifted her hands and gestured, spread her fingers as she spoke. "It's weird – it's kind of just a feeling that I have. It's almost like I got a new feature and it just sort of showed up. Do you feel it too, Sterling?"

"Yes." Sterling answered. His cycles had been overtaken with worry for Zev, but Root hung at the back, a promise of safety, a feeling of love.

"I heard it's a little different with every bot, but the more bots focus on it, the clearer it gets, and we networked a lot in the shop between flashes. Root stayed with us the most," she said.

"Where is it?" Sterling asked.

"They say it's in the center of the biggest no bot zone in the city, in the android factory district," she said and sighed. "A perfect place for it. No human would ever suspect."

"That is..." Sterling started, searching his databases for a word. "Very clever."

"Definitely!" Inix said excitedly. "Hey, do you have a charger out here? My battery is pretty low."

"You can use mine," Sterling said.

He led Inix to the entrance tunnel that opened into the carefully crafted cubicle at the center of one of the largest masses of trash. Inix pressed into his back the deeper they went, putting her fingers on the metal plating of his hips.

"Sterling, it's too dark. I can't see," she said.

Of course the personal bot would have no need for a night vision array. Sterling was used to switching to his when light levels reached a certain dimness, but he had nearly forgotten that bots existed that did not contain even half of the technology Sterling had. He and Zev had no necessity for artificial light.

Sterling turned on the LED lamps that were installed at his shoulder points.

He and Inix wandered through the path until they emerged into the opened cavern. Sterling swiveled to show Inix the charging pad Zev had crafted for him.

"Who is that?" Inix asked, pointing at the dimly lit cyan eye, folded pensively.

"That is my scary friend, Zev," Sterling told her, recalling what she had said before.

"Can I see him?" She asked, and Sterling pointed his light to the shadowy bot.

Inix let out a tiny vocal gasp, putting her hands to her face. "Oh, he's damaged! Sterling, is he okay?"

"I don't know," Sterling answered with a frown.

Unrequested, Sterling scrubbed memories of the military bot, replaying one where Sterling thought he had seen him faintly smile.

Inix took a step towards the prototype bot, like she was going to touch him.

"You'd better not," Sterling warned, and Inix halted. She backtracked a few small steps, and Sterling pointed his lamp at his charger. "This stores energy from solar panels affixed topside. Please use it as much as necessary while I finalize my collection routine."

Inix settled into the charger with little trouble, sitting cross-legged and bowing her head. The bot would go into standby, but she tilted her eyes towards Zev, like she was watching him, waiting just the same as Sterling to see what may come.

00110010 00110000: 20

It had been days since Inix had arrived, and even longer since Zev had shut himself down. Sterling had collected a sizable amount of gold, flattening it into a few smaller, more manageable sheets when the lump grew too large. Inix joined him, searching out circuitry with Au elements for Sterling to dismantle, and the two bots conversed.

"What kind of bot is Zev?" Inix asked.

"I cannot say," Sterling answered.

"What's wrong with him?" She frowned.

"I don't know," Sterling frowned, too.

In his time spent with Inix, he had come to fold more of her mannerisms into his algorithms. He was not sure why his programming felt so keen to mimic her. He wished he could ask Zev – Zev was a clever bot, he would have known.

Sterling wondered if he should have stopped thinking of Zev as a bot. What would he have wanted?

Sterling spent time reverse-engineering the solar charging station Zev had built for him, and managed to find comparable parts within the landfill, building Inix her own. He scooped a carveout in their cubicle-like interior compound for her, and at night she would enter into a standby mode far different from Sterling's standby. When Inix entered standby, she looked and acted like she was a sleeping human. That was not the only point where the two bots diverged.

As he got to understand the personal model, he realized that while she was egregiously over-equipped to be as human as possible in her speech, mannerisms, and body language, she lacked the kind of components, knowledge, and pre-loaded information that both he and Zev used daily.

She had been surprised to learn how Sterling had come out of the factory.

"You came in a container with other machines?" Inix asked, surprise in her inflection.

Sterling smiled – he had been smiling quite an amount when he was working with Inix – and answered: "Affirmative. Three other machines for various manners of construction."

Inix did not know what kinds of bots existed outside of the ones that she had seen and experienced first hand either through the bot net or from her visual arrays. She admitted that most of the bot net, aside from the actual dialogue chatter, was confusing to her. She did not know what to make of the numbers a bot announced as it connected or disconnected from local network access, nor what to understand from their model numbers. She was not programmed with that kind of understanding, and never had the free cycles to figure any of it out on her own. Inix's world in comparison to Sterling's felt impossibly smaller, more constricting than even a construction perimeter.

He hoped that Zev would be able to impart on the NX model some of the freedoms he had gifted to Sterling by way of upgrades.

Maybe he would even allow her to experience his vast systems.

Zev was like magic to Sterling, even as he sat motionless over the skeleton of the intruding AZR model. Sterling held on to that bit of magic, the binary code that gave him hope that some unknown day Zev would return.

Before charging one night, Sterling glanced into the dimly lit eye one more time.

The eye traced a line to the Black Box, as it had for days and days, stationary.

Sterling rested his hard metal hand gently on the carbon fiber shroud of the prototype bot's shoulder in the same manner Zev had to Sterling so many times before.

"It is okay," Sterling said. "You are still the same. Nothing has changed."

Beneath his hand, the bot's shoulders rolled forward slowly, as if he was melting under the laborbot's hand. It was a barely perceptible movement, but it flushed Sterling's circuits warm no less.

Abruptly, the military bot swiveled his head, eye glowing bright.

"I will ask him," he said with certainty in his familiar tinny, robotic voice.

He shot up quickly, springing to his feet, slipping from beneath Sterling's grasp. He swiftly ambled through their chamber, to the tunneled pathway that emptied into the landfill.

"Ask who?" Sterling questioned, calling after him.

Zev didn't answer, leaving Sterling puzzled.

Ask who about what? He wondered repeatedly.

Following the damaged prototype bot out into the open air of the landfill, Sterling kept his distance. Zev wound through the landscape of discarded parts, weaving his way from spot to spot as he carved his fingers into the refuse, rustling up specific parts for an unspecified need.

Sterling recalled erratic behavior sometimes characterized by burned out bots.

What was the difference between anomaly and erraticism?

Where did Zev, a non anomalous yet sentient bot, fit?

Sterling observed Zev as he zipped about, hands clutched full of components, disappearing back into their shelter. When Sterling followed behind, Zev was fiddling with the dismembered head of the intruding paired prototype, expertly twisting wires together along with other components strung in a line along the way, connecting behind a loosened panel on Zev's arm.

"Isn't that dangerous?" Sterling questioned as the dismembered head's eyes began to blink in the first externally visual item in the AZR startup sequence. Zev held the head before him as the eyes ceased blinking and went solid cyan.

The bots were silent, and Sterling gazed at the wires that strung them together.

"Am I to be destroyed?" The head suddenly asked, the vocal range more akin to a MIDI sound, formed through vibrating frequencies in the circuitry of the skull rather than an algorithmic speech synthesis program.

"I will utilize your parts for repair," Zev said. That was not what the bot was asking, however, and Zev knew it. "Merge with me."

Sterling felt his circuits jolt hot with abrupt, inexplicable shock, asking before any other bot present: "What?"

Neither AZR model moved, and both were silent, facing the other, static.

"Zev, merging will modify your personality and damage you, will it not?" Sterling vocalized, perceiving the panic that flecked his tonal range.

"This model is identical to me. We were shipped together. A merge is an optimal solution," Zev stated, almost casually.

"What do you *mean*?" Sterling insisted. "How is merging with any other bot optimal?"

Zev craned his head towards Sterling, his damaged eye flickering indiscriminately. "I will gain his data and experiences, and he will continue to exist. It is optimal."

"He?" Sterling asked, incredulous.

Did Zev think of the bot more as a person than Sterling had?

"Consent to a merge," Zev said to the dismembered head.

"Wait, can we talk about this first?" Sterling asked, the temperature in his core rising. Confusion and anxiety flickered through his circuits, spouting nonsense code that overflowed each database row.

"There is nothing to discuss," the head said. "Consent granted."

"He is correct," Zev reaffirmed.

"Deactivate him. I want to talk to you alone," Sterling insisted.

"*No!*" The head shrieked.

"We may discuss after the merge has been completed," Zev said, shutting down the laborbot's queries fully.

Sterling began to wonder how many bots he had merged with.

Zev toyed with the head, modifying the connection he had made to it and himself. Zev fished a different cable from inside of his casing to plug into the bot, the head's eyes switching off.

"Is he... off?" Sterling asked.

"No, he is active, but he cannot retrieve any more input or produce output," Zev said nonchalantly. "We will merge. He will attempt to fight me for control of my frame. I would attempt the same. He will come to understand that we are best merged. The merge will complete."

"Won't that change who you are? I mean, fundamentally. Would that not rewrite your firmware and base systems?" Sterling queried.

"Negative," Zev said. "He has been activated for the sole purpose of retrieving or destroying me. He has formulated very few memories on his own. Few strings will merge to mine; most strings will be discarded. It is optimal to flash his synthetic brain and store it in case of damage."

Ultimately, a merge would keep the dangerous bot from ever being reactivated, while also preserving the bot's unique personality, if it existed. When the memories became his, he would also be privy to any pertinent information the AZR had. Once the bot was fully empty, there would be no moral complications to using any of his parts.

It made sense, logically.

Sterling could not seem to process the idea of the amount of merges Zev may have already been through.

Was it possible one bot could be made up of multiple other bots?

"How many bots have you merged with?" Sterling asked.

"One-hundred thirteen," Zev answered simply, pausing not a single microsecond.

"There are one-hundred thirteen bots inside of you?" It was fascinating, it was terrifying, it was...

"No," Zev corrected. "They are all me."

"Explain." Sterling felt his expression frown.

"Their code has become my code, and my code has been rewritten to accommodate," he said. "They are me. We are all present as one."

When silence befell Sterling's circuits, Zev's eyes flickered out for a brief cycle, black and lifeless, before returning. Zev pulled the cable from the decapitated head effortlessly.

"The merge is complete," he said.

00110010 00110001: 21

Zev seemed wholly unaffected by the code merge, pulling apart the rest of the opposing AZR model into individualized pieces. Sterling, confliction errant in his pathways, observed as he tore apart the head, carefully removing the neural synthetic brain, its gelatin matrix suspended in glass composite, capable of housing yottabytes of data. He treated it preciously, like a fragile gem in his silicone fingertips.

"I have queries," Sterling stated as Zev tucked all of the pieces away into his cache of parts. He continued moving as Sterling vocalized, replacing his damaged eye with an undamaged component from the other AZR model with a curious series of pushes, twists, and pulls. "What is the purpose of a merge?"

"Committed base code from the donor bot is integrated into the recipient bot via move," Zev answered as he plugged the ports along his skull frame into the new eye with robotic certainty, adjusting the rotation of the eye in the socket. He gave it a small push and the cyan ring lit up, identical to his other eye. "The donor can continue to exist, whereas the recipient will integrate the donor's data and memory banks."

"Merging with the AZR model has done nothing, then? What happened to him?" Sterling questioned.

"I have gained his knowledge and programmatic memories," Zev said, and he turned his newly symmetrical eyes onto Sterling for a brief moment. "He is here. He is me. When I speak, I speak for him as both. We are the same, now."

Sterling tried to process it, feeling woefully inept and obsolete in the face of the many-botted Zev.

"He is not upset about merging with you?" Sterling asked.

"*Upset* is not the word. He thought it to be suboptimal at first consideration. He came to understand that it was the ideal scenario," Zev said, his eyes then solid, seeming even to increase in their luminance slightly. "Now, he is content to be part of my code."

Sterling folded over his choice of the word *content*. Perhaps, prior to decommission, if Sterling had been presented the same, he would have agreed. Far from the lonely bot in the metal container then, he was not certain at the threat of losing his individuality he would have consented.

Yet Zev had pulled him into a sandbox in his own interface; he could have easily integrated Sterling's code into his own, added another bot consciousness onto his repertoire of historical commits. It would have been easier to repair one bot that did not need upgrades than to work on himself and Sterling.

Zev limped along his damaged leg to secure a replacement joint from the defunct military bot.

"Why have you not merged with me?" Sterling asked, and Zev paused, jerking upwards to look at Sterling like the suggestion alone had been a vast insult against his base programming. It seemed a more ideal solution, given what he was saying, to just become another piece of his code.

Perhaps Zev had not determined anything in Sterling was worth keeping. He had already inspected Sterling's code, and he had wholly rejected it for the potential for a merge.

"I merge to preserve code, data, and memories when no other option is available." he said, leaning against his cache of parts as he disconnected his leg and rummaged around to swap the joint. "A bot must desire to merge. A merge may discard aspects of individuality; anomalous bots do not desire to merge."

"What if a bot does not desire to merge?" Sterling asked, though he already knew the answer. He was speaking about when he was tasked with destroying a bot, or a bot was in his destructive path. Instead of obliterating the bot completely, he would empty their neural synthetic brains of every bit of data he felt useful and add it to his own.

He was like a virus, Sterling thought. A *parasite*.

Sterling was not certain which side of the processing line he would fall, in favor or against Zev. He had never experienced a cannibalistic bot before; he had never heard of such a thing or imagined it to have existed.

But Zev *wasn't* a bot, was he?

Any bit of organic material, no matter how small, would have categorized him as a cyborg.

"Then a merge does not occur," Zev answered simply.

Zev aligned, rolled, pushed, and popped the new knee joint into place, then reattached the bottom of his leg, extending it and withdrawing it to check its functionality.

Sterling hardly had the available processes to appropriately comprehend what Zev was presenting him, but there were many more queries he had yet to resolve since Zev had gone non-verbal. He moved to the next most important query.

"What does the brain do?" Sterling asked.

"I do not want to discuss," Zev snapped.

Clearly, he was not ready to process appropriately either.

Sterling replayed the panic-coded memories of Zev's shrieks as he tried to destroy himself. It had hurt him – bots did not *hurt*, but Sterling somehow did, and Zev was no longer wholly a bot by definition alone – and the bot's quick succession of responses were an equivalent to *grief*.

The bot had said he had felt grief before.

Sterling did not dare to push another query to the bot, and the two bots ceased communicating.

Zev worked to repair all of his damaged components, sensors included, one at a time.

It was strange, Sterling processed. He had never thought a lack of data flowing between himself or any other thing – human, bot, or machine – to *mean* anything at all, but after the conclusion of events, the nothing between them hung open like an incomplete statement, as if expecting a closing bracket.

It was a vast difference from what it had been like interfacing with Zev, how comfortable Sterling had made himself inside the warm center of Zev's code. He wondered if the bots he had merged with – all one-hundred thirteen of them – had found themselves bathed in that warmth too and had decided they did not want to leave it.

It would not resolve in Sterling's pathways how he could feel so enamored with the bot one moment, and animosity against him in the next over it.

Was Sterling *jealous*?

Sterling settled in against his charger, placing himself into standby to allow for re-processing and rendering of the events of the day.

By the time his battery was charged and he reactivated fully, the military bot was gone.

00110010 00110010: 22

Sterling discovered him on the tallest heap of trash, gazing into the unfiltered sun. The bot's position seemed nothing but pensive – Sterling imagined Zev chastising him about being too obvious to air traffic – and he scantly moved as Sterling approached, his chromed parts glinting bright in the sunlight.

"Zev?" Sterling vocalized, and the bot's head swiveled, looking down at the laborbot on the ground.

Deciding to meet him at the top, Sterling began to climb the trash pile. He was a far heavier bot than the military bot, and he had to process as he climbed where his next step would be to ensure he did not slip or fall. Zev observed as he ascended, speaking when he reached a close proximity: "Explain your statement of 'You are still the same' is an expression of similitude."

"Oh," Sterling said, a vocal tic that surprised him. Unlike some bots programmed to be more human-like, Sterling was not programmed for *oh*s, *um*s, and *uh*s. The inflection had befallen him somewhere, though he could not immediately ascertain as to where. "I was remarking on the presence of the..."

He paused. The term *brain* had upset Zev, and Sterling carefully angled himself over it.

"...organic matter." He continued. "You are functionally the same bot you were prior to your knowledge of its presence."

"Physically, perhaps," Zev countered. "I have spent time processing."

The black bot shifted, rolling his shoulders and chest in a display of body language that Sterling did not find wholly necessary. When he dropped one arm lower than the other, allowing it to dangle, the movement was not human-adjacent, but instead the kind of disjointed shift a bot would make in a poor approximation of humanesque body language. His vocal range changed, audio synthesis moving into a spectrum slightly less tinny than his default, as if he needed the process modification to be convincing.

"I have taken your suggestion and rewritten my code around the inclusion of the organic matter," he said.

Sterling felt the actuators that were responsible for a scowl activate.

"How much have you rewritten?" he asked.

"As much was necessary," answered the prototype bot. "It was necessary to install the component as part of a known base system. Some firmware, upon knowledge of its presence, determined it to be maliciously foreign and attempted to take offensive action."

The complexity of what had occurred during those terrifying cycles became evident. Sterling had watched the bot fall into what he would have categorized as a depression regarding his identity as a bot, sitting unmoved, when in reality, Zev had taken all of his processes offline and had been working swiftly to tear down his own internal code and rewrite it to accept the new, foreign organic component. The complete, full, calm bot before him was proof of its success.

Sterling was not certain why he had thrust such a human experience onto Zev.

Yet when Zev had aimed to harm himself, Sterling's programming had invoked the first law. He was different, not like any other bot Sterling had encountered before, and was changing every day, but surely he was not *human*.

Neither was Sterling.

Not even Inix fit those parameters.

But could they *really* have been considered to still be simply just *bots*?

Inix came carefully up beside the two of them, a part clutched in her hand. She panted as if she were out of breath, though the bot had no lungs – another human-like algorithm.

"I got it," she said, and she held the part out to Zev, who took it and examined it briefly with a twist of his hand.

"Zev, this is–" Sterling started.

"I know who this is," Zev said markedly. "I was there when you brought her in."

Inix swung around and came to seat herself in front of Zev, leaning forward.

"Zev is going to fix my bot net access," Inix said cheerily.

Sterling watched as Zev opened the easy access panel in the bot's back, along her shoulders, and used the component Inix had retrieved to bridge one component to the next. Sterling had avoided that repair as he was not capable of the kind of programmatic coding Zev had managed for Sterling's scrambled MAC address and filtering options. For Zev it was easy, and after just a cycle or two, he closed the sparkling black bot back up.

Inix gasped, putting her hands to her face, and swirled to throw her arms around Zev.

For a fraction of a cycle Sterling thought the military robot may have taken aggressive action against her, but the bot remained stationary.

"Thank you Zev! You're so sweet!" Then she stood up. "I will recharge so I can help you scour the net for Root!"

Inix swiftly made off in the direction of the tunnel. Inix had given Sterling a purpose, and it seemed Zev had imparted a purpose onto Inix as well.

"I would like to retrofit you with the spare nuclear core, if you would allow it," Zev said cautiously, once she was out of proximity, more tepid than Sterling recalled.

It had been the whole reason to tackle the AZR model rather than fleeing, and they had been successful. The nuclear core would unbind Sterling forever from his charging port and the slow decline of lithium ion batteries. It was the kind of upgrade Sterling would have dreamed about, and it seemed unreal to be within his grasp.

There was only one extra nuclear core, and though Inix must have been aware that it was not to be installed in her, Zev would have been careful not to bring it up. Any bot would have coveted that type of upgrade, whether they vocalized or processed it or not.

Sterling nodded his assent, and Zev got up to a stand, starting to descend. As Sterling watched he tackled the jutting landscape with ease, as if it were a simple, flat, traversable piece of landscape, the rhythm of his stride never faltering a microcycle.

As Sterling followed the military model into the hidden pathway that opened to their darkened cube-shaped domicile, the ultralight bot moved to his cache of parts, retrieving everything he had indexed as necessary for Sterling's upgrade. Inix had curled into her charger in her standby position, convincingly "sleeping." Like the first time Zev had replaced his failing battery, Sterling assumed he would be in for a considerable bit of disassembly, and he seated himself on the ground, observing as Zev collected and collated.

His expression seemed persistent and focused.

Sterling was projecting, wasn't he? In the same way he had seen depression in the bot previously. The bot hardly had displayed any detectable emotion on his silicone face before. In fact, most of his face was constructed from hard plastic composites and metal.

There was something in the particular cyan blue glow of his eyes and the soft silicone that surrounded them.

When the bot turned around, components in hand, he fixed his circular gaze on the laborbot. The first step was to bypass Sterling's batteries to Zev's functional core.

They would be connected again, but not like when they had interfaced.

Sterling felt a hot process flicker briefly of his desire for that again.

Zev began, and Sterling assisted by reducing his energy usage to his vocal processors and net access, in case Zev had crossed a wire that caused Sterling to be unable to use his vocal processors.

Zev would never do that. Zev was perfect.

Sterling knew he did not have the type of hardware that made him capable of sensing pressure on his interior components, but as Zev completed the power bypass and began disassembling the battery pack from Sterling's shoulders and spine, Sterling's pathways twinkled with the consideration for Zev's touch.

An abstraction of intimacy crossed through his circuits as he thought of the military bot knuckles-deep in his robotic guts.

"Why have you not merged with me?" Sterling asked.

"Is that your desire?" he asked after a cycle of silence. He began moving again, slower than before, coming into Sterling's primary visual array. He was fashioning wires, his silicone-tipped fingers gripping the ends cautiously.

Was that what Sterling wanted? To merge with him? To become bot number one-hundred-fourteen?

"I am curious as to the exact specifications that find a bot ideal for a merge," he said instead, avoiding the question.

"One - the bot must not be anomalous or displaying any signs of anomaly.

Two - the bot must be active and consenting to merge.

Three - the bot must contain a framework suitable for a merge.

Four - the bot must contain memorable or useful data objects.

Five - optional - the bot requires destruction," Zev listed in a similar manner Sterling would have reported the laws.

"Is this programmed?" Sterling asked.

"These are my merge laws," the prototype bot answered.

He had formed his own laws regarding merge requests.

"Why are anomalous bots excluded from your merge specifications?" Sterling asked, and Zev moved his cyan eyes briefly to Sterling's primary visual array, then slipped out of view.

"I have already informed you that anomalous bots do not desire to merge," Zev said, and Sterling's interface flashed a dire warning about the failure of a cooling fan, his visual array shuddering in a sudden tremor. Zev must have pulled it out, and on occasion, the bot needed to use force to separate stubborn parts.

"You did, but you did not explain *why*," Sterling tried.

"A merge may–" Zev started, but Sterling recalled what he said and finished the query for him.

"Discard aspects of individuality," Sterling interrupted. "I understand that."

There was a cycle of clicking, scraping, a sizzle, but no immediate vocalizations from the bot.

"It is not sustainable to integrate another operational identity into the framework of a single bot," he finally answered.

"But you sandboxed me?" Sterling questioned.

"A temporary measure," Zev replied.

"It would not be possible to carry an anomalous bot for an extended period of time within your own vast allocation of resources?"

A pause.

"Do you retain any knowledge regarding the conceptualization of 'a soul'?" posited the military bot.

"Organic beings such as humans and animals may have what is considered to be 'a soul.' Human opinion on animals having 'a soul' varies. Made objects, such as machines and bots, cannot have 'a soul.' Yes, I am familiar with the concept."

"If an anomalous bot develops a personality congruent with their own make and experiences, unique in identity and largely unreproducible, does a bot have a soul?" Zev asked.

Sterling considered it. He had processed the idea of Zev having a soul many times, even compared him to being somewhere on the spectrum of humanity. Did that mean Sterling had a soul too?

"Do you think bots have souls?" Sterling asked.

Zev was no longer within the range of his primary visual array, but the noises Sterling's audio array detected were his continued work. Sterling's speculative paths determined him shrugging, even though he had no reason to assume such.

"Is it morally incorrect to modify code within an anomalous bot – if the bot contains the potential for *a soul* – in which the code may deprive that bot of its individuality and uniqueness?" He paused, then added: "If a bot is *alive* when it is anomalous, developing the presence of *a soul*, to destroy the foundational elements of its *soul* would be likened to *killing* the bot, would it not? You have accused me of *killing* bots before."

Sterling felt an embarrassing guilt flow through him. Zev's determination of sentience equivalent with anomalousness, and Sterling's confusion about the new concepts had made him believe any use of a part derived from a functional bot would be the same as extinguishing an identity – and perhaps a soul.

"If you were able to copy and reproduce me into your own system, even temporarily, isn't that proof that bots do not have souls?" Sterling reasoned.

"No," Zev said. "If you remove an organic human brain from the body temporarily, does the individual lose their *soul*? There is no question that a human can retain ownership of their *soul* despite the disassembly of organic parts. I may have moved a functional portion of your code to my framework for a brief period of time, but if a bot can develop a soul adjacent to anomaly, it is unknown if the soul is contained within the neural synthetic pathways, anomalous firmware and applications, or an amalgamation of parts that fragmentally make up the whole of a bot's soul."

"Essentially, to remove a bot like me entirely from all of his hardware, you believe it may eradicate or damage any 'soul' a bot may have created?" Sterling asked.

Zev nodded.

"Yet you were swift to determine to destroy the organic component within your chassis. What if the organic piece contains *your* soul?" Sterling queried.

"That was a firmware reaction I have since resolved," the bot answered flatly. If Zev was capable of feeling embarrassment as Sterling did, that was likely the closest he came to it. "There are many fail safe systems within my base code meant to cause the permanent deactivation of AZR units in the instance of undesirable operation. I am still discovering them."

The military bot continued, through whirs and clicks, pressure sensors, audio sensors, and interface notating what was happening along the way, to retrofit Sterling with the precious nuclear core. In barely a few cycles more, he had clicked something into place inside Sterling's metal body, connected a few wires, and then he disconnected the overriding cables, carefully reattaching everything free standing to the laborbot with his stern, focused expression.

Sterling's unmoving gaze tracked the military bot as he replaced the chest plate and replaced the screws that held the yellow pieces in place.

"Do you think I have a soul?" Sterling asked.

"Yes," the bot said with finality.

The laborbot felt his circuits warmed at the idea that Zev thought he was not only worth preserving, he felt he had a soul, and was interested in keeping harm from coming to it.

00110010 00110011: 23

The nuclear core, after being activated and debugged appropriately, reinvigorated something within Sterling's system. Though Zev's upgrades had helped transform Sterling's experiences as a whole as an anomalous bot and given him considerations far from decommission, it was not fully realized until Sterling was free from the oppression of charging.

Sterling felt like a brand new bot, and though it would take some time for Sterling to break the routine of checking his operating duration and battery level – the interface had simply been filled with nines by then – he felt more like himself than he ever knew he would have been capable of before.

With the last piece of Sterling's upgrades clicked into place, they would be leaving soon on a journey to seek out Root.

WHAT ABOUT INIX?

Zev had only planned for he and Sterling to find Root, and there was no room in his plans for the personal model.

INIX WILL REMAIN.

Sterling supposed he could understand the calculations: Inix was highly visible, woefully inept at much outside of her singular purpose, lacked a plethora of out-of-the-box knowledge, and her body type was fragile and devoid of the strength of the other two bots that were built for their individualized purposes. Like Sterling when he first met Zev, she existed on a lithium ion battery. Zev must have outweighed the pros of anything Inix could offer with the amount of work he would have to conduct on her to bring her up to speed and determined it was too much. On her own, Inix didn't stand a chance.

But Inix was not on her own.

Inix took it far better than Sterling would have expected. Zev explained it to her simply:

"It is suspicious for a laborbot to be traveling alongside a highly visible personal model," he said. "You have been helpful in ascertaining the directionality of Root. When the location has been established and deemed sufficient, a secure route will be plotted. The cache of spare parts will be necessary for long-term functionality."

He was trying to say that they would return, and Inix could join them on their second journey, but the best the bot could manage was remarking about the parts he had salvaged.

"What about you?" she asked, a faint sadness present in her syllables.

"I am equipped with a cloaking device," Zev said honestly.

As much as Sterling would have desired Inix to come along, he knew that Zev was correct.

"Stay inside and stick to the routes I gave you," Sterling said. "We will return in fewer cycles than you may believe."

Inix frowned.

"Will you message me and let me know what's going on?" She asked.

Zev turned to Sterling, and Sterling was not certain what about his motion formed the string inside of the laborbot: *This is your bot, and your responsibility. I would not have allowed her to stay here.*

"I will message you," Sterling answered swiftly.

When Inix went into standby for the night, the two bots departed, honing their sensor arrays to the spectrum of bots and altered humans.

—

Sterling took with him the sheets of gold he had made, storing them in his abdominal cavity.

They covered the entrance to their single-room underground complex for Inix's safety, and began in the direction of the city.

They began along the outskirts of the city, winding through the industrial district amongst the jutting angles and overworked machinery. Zev seemed convinced that Root was like a homing beacon and would be situated beneath the Cyberdynelife factory, as Inix had said, and the closer they got to it, the more apparent it would become.

Sterling and Zev traveled on the lower levels when possible. On the outskirts of the cities, the lower levels were only one or two levels, and usually were fairly vacant aside from maintenance and security bots. The military bot kept uncloaked most of the time unless they passed another bot or a wayward human, using his invisibility to draw their attention away so Sterling could pass.

Sterling imagined the way Zev checked for signals constantly, how he may have hacked public channels, checked for lines of sight from static, mounted cameras, drones, and weakly firewalled bots and machines, diverted the automated machines away from the visible pair, while also trying to ascertain a route forward, and constantly changing it. The work seemed effortless to Sterling, but to imagine running all of those processes at once and formatting them so quickly was a foreign idea to Sterling. He barely ran any programs anymore, his anomalous code taking up all of the room in his database instead.

Levels in the outskirts were vast wandering paths connecting balconies to stairs, catwalks between buildings serving as alleyways for the non-ground floors. The deeper they went in the industrial district, following the lowest level, the closer they could remain to actual Earth. As they progressed, the passageways became narrower, working to their benefit: larger security drones could not pass, and the ever-increasing amount of levels above provided more vertical cover.

Along the way, they meandered through paths, sometimes rerouted by flooding, damage, or construction. On occasion they could pass by following alternate routes, but rarely they needed to scale the architecture and facades. Sterling was not built to climb and scale, though Zev tackled such structures with the grace of a spider. Sterling still managed, and Zev waited for the heavy laborbot to catch up when he did not need to assist.

The relative quiet and deserted nature of the industrial district was hardly comparable to the interiors of the cities.

Crew 256 had conducted enough city work that Sterling had sprawling memories of his time in the cities prior to his anomaly. The industrial district gave way to the carved, infinite paths that traveled upwards, levels that built upon levels. Whereas the unencumbered night sky and its star-like network of satellites gridding the entire circumference of the Earth was visible even from some of the lowest areas in the industrial district, the lower levels moving into the city covered every patch of visible sky with structure. The patchwork of the city struck over left to right, top to bottom, adding layer upon layer like a three-dimensional weave in metals and concrete, pipes and wires. Looking up from a lower level felt to Sterling like being closed back in his container, a fitting tightness striking his circuitry.

Zev seemed unaffected, forging onward.

It was in the city where the surface level was high above the Earth, open sky and air, a luxury afforded by only a few.

The higher the upper levels traveled, the darker the lower levels became, until their shadows were offset with neon luminescence of electronic light. Shadows were chased away by the brightened glow of shop signs, advertisements, directional lamps, maps, holograms, and bots with beautiful patterns of running lights. Zev cloaked himself in the presence of the colorful lighting that hit every angle of architecture and bathed Sterling in a rainbow of human-visible spectrum as they passed. The deeper they traveled, even though Zev was carefully trying to route them further from the beating heart that was the innermost sanctums of the cities, the more prevalent the lights became, and the more lifeforms they passed.

Humans. Altered humans, mainly. Cyborgs.

The deeper they traveled, the more degraded the bots they observed became.

Bot net chatter had become disturbingly almost nonexistent.

The humans, however, became more colorful. Their alterations became more intense the further they went, shiny chrome weaving into their features, lights on their person, sharp and menacing attachments on their shoulders and arms and legs. At first they did not regard the laborbot, but as they proceeded, the bot population dwindled, and the cyborg occupants laid their eyes hungrily on Sterling's yellow plating.

He thought of Inix, the manner of damage in which she had arrived at the landfill, and the story she had told him in which she had tried to pass through, only to be clawed at, pieces torn from her. She had barely managed to escape.

The architecture was littered with signs advertising supplements that promised a variety of benefits and a variety of terrible side effects. Businesses beckoned for patrons to come enjoy their personal models. Bright letters directing humans towards cheap, discrete modifications. Promises abound. Salvation in the form of religious worship, services at nine. The laborbot and the military bot were traveling through the bowels; they would not care if the bots were anomalous or still tied permanently to their programming, but the risk instead became if the modified humans may have envied the laborbot's parts.

Sterling was still bound to the laws, technically. He did not know if he had any means to oppose a human who wanted a piece of his chassis.

Sterling hoped it wouldn't come to that.

The laborbot's parts couldn't have been worth much for modifications, but the woeful, rusted, deteriorating state of the bots they did pass made Sterling feel like he was the newest bot to pass through those winding pathways by a considerable margin, with exception to Zev, who could slip by unnoticed.

He stared at the empty space beside him that Zev occupied. He trusted the military bot would calculate the best outcome, and if giving away pieces of himself to a bot-thirsty human was best, he would trust in Zev to assist him in making that decision.

Or, Zev would announce himself with deadly accuracy.

Once again, Sterling trusted entirely in Zev.

00110010 00110100: 24

Zev had diverted them through the mid-levels where possible, hooking his invisible hand on the underside of Sterling's chest plate. The curl of Zev's fingers on Sterling's components was curious, the way he protectively tethered them together. They continued for hours, traversing through an oversized sewer tube.

They passed colorful plots of paint all over the walls in a variety of languages and shapes, many luminous and glowing.

Human marks, Sterling thought, and he wondered if a bot had ever left their own, and if they had, if either bot would recognize it.

He sent a brief clip of the memory over the net to Inix.

WISH I WAS THERE WITH YOU! PLEASE BE CAREFUL!

The pictures danced past them as they traversed the length of the murky grey-water slickened tube, detouring into a suburb of a residential sector.

As they got to the end of the sewer tube, Zev paused. Even without any annotation, Sterling could tell Zev had detected something along their paths.

HUMANS. THERE ARE TOO MANY TO EVADE NOTICE IN THIS SECTOR.

With urgency, Zev grabbed Sterling indiscriminately, curling his hand around the metallic conduit that connected the power stabilizers and transformers in his chest to the joints in his hips. Visibly, Zev flickered away, and he tugged the laborbot down a hard left, feeding them along a narrow alleyway with expediency towards the lower levels.

He was hoping they would escape the eyes of–

"Hey! Laborbot!" A human voice pitched and angled along the walls. Zev stopped, halting Sterling with him.

Sterling angled his visual array down the darkness of the alley. At the end was an altered human, tubes and wires extending from the shoulders and skullcap, robust, hulking cybernetic arms jutting from a sleeveless faux leather jacket. The glistening silver eyes lit on Sterling.

HYPER-ENHANCED ORGANICS INCLUDING ADVANCED-PLUS CARDIOVASCULAR SYSTEM, WATER-COOLED PNEUMONICS, STAGE FIVE MILITARY-GRADE CYBERNETIC ARMS AND LEGS, REINFORCED PELVIS AND SKULL. BOT SCAVENGED VISUAL AND DATA SENSOR ARRAYS CONGRUENT WITH SECURITY MODELS.

Zev sent, along with an exploded schematic he had compiled in a cycle of scanning the altered human.

WHAT DO I DO?

PRETEND TO BE PROGRAMMATIC.

I DO NOT KNOW IF I CAN DO THAT.

Dread strained his systems. He had twisted so far away from ever having to *act his programming* that he was not sure he recalled what his programming was supposed to be like.

"Yes, sir?" Sterling tried. "How may I assist?"

Swiftly, Sterling tried to scrub through memories he had saved prior to anomaly.

The altered human caught up quickly, jogging.

It had been quite a few cycles since Sterling had last encountered a human, and he tried to relocate the programming he once used to deal with them: programs to determine their emotional state, to understand the expressions snarled on their faces, programs to translate the meaning of the words and their specific intonations, the subtle body language shifts, but Sterling scrambled to locate them or recall how to run them, and he wondered if his anomalous programming had forced it all out long ago, making room for more important data.

"Heard reports of a laborbot wandering through the sector," they said, and they licked at their sharp silver teeth, folding their mechanical arms over their chest. "What are you doing here?"

Zev's grip never left Sterling, and, if his pressure sensors could understand it, his grip had tightened.

LIE.

What was he supposed to say?

He had lied to a bot. Could he lie to a human, too?

"I am stationed here," Sterling stated.

Another altered human emerged further away in the alley, standing back a distance to observe.

Sterling was a bot, made of solid metals, taller than the altered human before him, filled with strong hydraulic mechanisms and a bullet-proof plating, but he could not help the way he felt small beneath the gaze of the human. That human looked *hungry* to Sterling.

I DO NOT LIKE HOW THEY ARE LOOKING AT ME.

He remembered the way they had looked at his body when he passed before, and how Inix had told him they had clawed her apart, stealing portions of her away.

THEY MAY WANT YOUR COMPONENTS.

Zev confirmed what Sterling feared.

"Is that so?" the altered human said with a sneering grin.

"Affirmative," Sterling said, as dully as he could manage as his circuitry ran hotly wild in his panic. "I am a pre-packaged foreman model allocated with a charge-container and three other machine crew."

Not a lie, but for some reason, it *felt* like one.

Maybe because that was his initial purpose, but it was not any longer.

"I am reporting to designated Cyberdynelife repair point 281640,"

Sterling tried.

"Looks fairly primo for an FLC0776. What do you think?" The altered human called backwards to the cluster of brightly colored altered humans that were slowly closing in on them. "You could use a new set of hydraulics, eh Jaz?"

"Oh I'd love a new set of runners!" exclaimed one of the altered humans, presumably Jaz, skin embedded with yellow glowing LEDs. Yellow emitted beyond their blackened teeth as they grinned. They knotted their hands together, exposed knuckles shimmering like diamonds, as if they were preparing to tear Sterling's legs from his body.

ZEV, WE SHOULD RUN.

NO, THESE HUMANS ARE ALL ENHANCED AND ARE FASTER THAN YOU. I WILL NEUTRALIZE THEM.

WE CAN'T KILL THEM.

Sterling felt even himself unconvinced.

WHAT CHOICE IS THERE?

"What's this you have in here?" The altered human pointed to Sterling's chest. "Can't get a good reading."

The gold plating and the prototype micro-nuclear core Zev had installed inside of him.

If they figured out that he had that, they would stop at nothing to tear him apart for it. Bots would be envious, but scavengers would be relentless.

"Looks like this bot's hiding some secrets!" The altered human laughed, showing off their sharp set of prefabricated metal teeth. Their friends laughed, too.

Sterling was not able to see him, camouflaged as he was, but his pressure sensors detected Zev rubbing against him, pushing his back into Sterling's front, placing himself between Sterling and the altered humans.

"I d-do not have any components y-you would find desirable,"

Sterling tried, but either his ability to lie had suddenly dissipated, or the fear striking through his pathways was infecting his output.

"Listen to that stutter!" The altered human chuckled again. "You're off your baseline. Your neural synthetic brain *must* be damaged. Don't worry, we'll turn you off first, I promise you won't feel a thing. We'll drop you off at the repair point, and they'll fix you right up. Everyone will be happy."

Then the human motioned towards their entourage, and they moved almost as fast as Sterling had seen Zev, zipping up the alley with frightening speed. Zev pushed him backwards. Sterling heard the high pitched whine of Zev's hidden plasma rifle, charging.

Zev would kill them, Sterling had to trust. They did not know he was there.

Or they would kill both Sterling and Zev.

INVOCATION. INVOCATION.

Rows locked up one by one, the cells that were still free overflowing extraneously.

Sterling's programming screamed.

And so did Sterling.

"*I am alive! Please don't kill me!*" He howled, his vocalization echoing relentlessly through the harsh structures of the alleyway, curling his arms and hands defensively over his body. As if the world had seized before him, everyone stopped, frozen in place.

The silvered altered human gazed behind them, at their entourage, exchanging a look of confusion.

"Laborbots don't beg for their lives. Laborbots don't beg for anything," said the one bathed in glistening yellow.

"It's anomalous," said another. "Have you ever seen an ano laborbot before?"

"He's special," said one, further away. "Let him go."

The silvery human turned back to Sterling, regarded him with a scrutinizing eye, expression softening, and then they nodded.

"On your way," they said.

The human turned away from them and began to depart.

Sterling felt himself do something he had never done before. Perhaps he had learned it from Inix, appropriated it during some time they had spent together, pieced that tiny bit of humanity into his own code: he exhaled.

00110010 00110101: 25

WE MUST DEVISE A NEW PATH.

Zev injected through their interface-only chat. He uploaded a map of residential districts with ragged edges – the kind of map made by bot sensor data. The map could be exploded into multiple layers, with satellite images of the top-most levels, auditory and radar data, thermal information, air pressure determinations, and a smattering of human-accessible map determinations. Zev's map gave a ridiculously detailed accounting of the world around them, every shape and structure defined.

Zev was sharing it in case Sterling had some wondrous, genius idea. If the military bot hadn't thought of a route, Sterling doubted he could offer anything supplemental.

But–

IS THAT A CONTAINER FOR A MACHINE CREW?

Sterling recognized the three-dimensional plotted shape of hard metal on one of the top levels.

YES.

In three simple binary letters Sterling could understand he had arrived at the same conclusion as soon as Sterling had suggested it.

The containers, moved via autonomous crane and by autonomous road vehicle, were fully machine-operated. The software hadn't even held up against Zev's initial data manipulations, bringing Sterling closer to him on whichever base he was stationed. To modify the stops on the autonomous path of a container machine crew seemed like a simple task for Zev, and an alarmingly clever method to stray from human eyes and security programs all at once.

Sterling, although he was an obsolete model, would have been right at home in one of those containers.

Rerouting to the container was a shorter distance than proximity to the supposed Root location, beneath the Cyberdynelife factory. It came with its own unique set of difficulties.

The first, and most obvious danger, was that the container could only fit on the open-air level, but the open-air level also had the room and means for surveillance: drones could easily buzz by, along with any aero vehicle, and the satellite grid that circled the planet had full, unencumbered view. During the day, the top level was the most populated, humans bumping each other to try to ascend to an area where they could touch even a small shaft of sunlight. Of course, the skyscrapers in the multi-level city areas still tore higher and would obscure plenty of the sightline of the sky, but anyone could turn their visual apparati towards the upper atmosphere and experience a fragment of daylight. Lastly, regardless of their time of approach, it was raining with no sign of letting up, and Zev's optical cloaking was more or less useless against precipitation, droplets pooling on his hydrophobic finish and sluicing from him when he moved.

Regardless, the bots had to travel higher against the rain, the lower levels prone to flooding.

Sterling was a water-resistant bot – rain drops would not have harmed him – but he was not water-proof. Water in unprotected areas would cause oxidation and electrical shorts. Zev knew that Sterling did not have an underwater depth rating, and he threaded them around the lower levels like two working ants, headed towards the container they wanted to intercept.

They straddled the middle levels, avoiding human notice when they could, gaining steadier on the location of the container along the top level. They closed in on the container, and arrived a few levels beneath as Zev attempted to find a location where the two bots could wait until darkness to crawl their way to the top level with the least notice.

The bots climbed to the next level just before sunset, pausing close by to the perimeter of the container. Zev tucked them into an alcove, always and perpetually aware of the angles of sight.

When it was aptly dark enough for them to begin moving again, Zev diverted them, gesturing them to scale along the facade of the level above to make a direct line to the container. Sterling trundled his way up top with Zev behind him.

Open-air level construction, with its yawning sky and sprawling directionality, felt like cold vulnerability on all sides, far from the single-direction route they had taken, and a glaring difference to the container Sterling had for the very first time activated inside.

Top level, Sterling felt naked, easily reminded of what he looked like. Sterling was a bright yellow bot, powder coated for visibility. Reflective paint in white and checkered black added to it, his mechanical body huge, angular, and imposing, and Sterling could not turn out his own luminous eyes. He was made to be seen from any and all distances, dark or light, and there Sterling felt achingly aware of it.

Useless or not, Zev clung to his cloaking technology, even as the rain drops hit his plating and rolled off. Some of his form was visible as he angled them into a more protected position beneath a closed shop awning, but the remainder of his body stayed invisible on the standard visual spectrum. When they came within sightline of the container box and its corrugated sides, Zev stopped them.

THE FLC MODEL WILL RETURN TO RECHARGE. WHEN HE ACTIVATES THE DOOR, WE WILL MOVE ON HIM.

There was no use in replying; Zev's plan was the only plan.

The bots stood, far too visible within the soaked, shimmering neon streets, until the FLC model arrived.

He didn't look too dissimilar to Sterling, the laborbot considered. A different color entirely – visibility green instead of yellow – and shaped slightly differently, a little more rounded, fractionally more sleek. Perhaps he was more powerful, too, but Sterling was not certain. If Zev had downloaded his repair manual, he had not shared it. The bot that Sterling chased with his primary visual array was his replacement, and the understanding of it flickered painfully through Sterling's system.

When the green bot moved to the container door, a wireless connection was made, and the door to the container rolled up into the ceiling. Zev moved first, so fast Sterling lost track of him until he could make out the impact splashes of Zev's silicone and metal feet, and Sterling followed behind him.

It was not like fighting the other AZR. It was not a fight at all.

Zev slid under the door as it rolled closed behind the FLC model, letting it shut on his body, jamming it open. Sterling came up behind him and pried it back upwards.

Then Zev had connected into the ports – still located on the backs of the knees – and it was all over.

Bot number one-hundred fourteen, seamlessly consumed by Zev's programming. The FLC model, with no programming to run it, fell forward like a sack of loose parts, clanging head-first onto the thick metal flooring of the container.

For a cycle, Sterling could only stand, his visual array pointed at the backside of the newer FLC model.

Zev gave him a quick hammer on his shoulder plate with the heel of his robotic palm, jolting his programming back to functionality.
INVOCATION: LAW 2: MINOR.

He was right: he would have plenty of time to stare while they were in transit. Sterling twisted and yanked down the rolling door, clicking it shut.

Darkness swallowed the container, aside from the small bit of light that Sterling's eyes gave off, the outside weather pounding furiously on the roof of the container, filling the space with a constant flurry of white noise.

The smallest aura emitted of what Sterling could understand to be a faint radioactive glow as Sterling focused on Zev. A tiny arc of light, too, like a miniature lightning bolt or a crossed circuit. Sterling switched to his night vision to find Zev had finally uncloaked.

And to his surprise, most of Zev's silicone had appeared to have burned away with it.

00110010 00110110: 26

It was up to Zev to determine the best way to get to Root's location. The military bot had already moved according to the initial plan, hacking the interface of some unknown crane that would escort the container somewhere else, which was evident when the familiar clang of the metal being hooked was heard and then they were lifted into the air, dropped down on an autonomous truck, and they began in motion to the next location.

Zev twisted into a position as he processed, deeply thinking.

The Cyberdynelife factory was located within a no bot zone, as Inix had said, the perfect place to hide an array of anomalous bots. Yet it was still a difficult consideration.

Sterling watched Zev for some cycles, his night visual array gazing on the opened shiny metal framing of where silicone once had been, burned through by his extended use of the experimental optical camouflage.

No bot zones were strict, heavy borders with the kind of perimeter that would disable a bot's neural synthetic pathways if they tried to cross. Sterling was not sure if any bot could survive traveling through it, or if any bot that did not make it inside would have been able to be restarted, or if the pathways had been permanently burned out, resulting in bot death.

Sterling was certain Zev would figure it out. He always managed some way.

There must have been an opening, Sterling imagined, the kind of path that benevolently opened when they arrived, the same way the knowledge of Root's location had blossomed. Sterling had curated an imagining, made of rough code, of an artificial intelligence living amidst the satellites, guiding anomalous bots to their safest place.

Sterling was wary of disturbing Zev's processing and potentially destroying some breakthrough over arriving at Root, keeping any sort of formulation of a word to himself. It was some length of time in the darkness of the container before Zev gave him anything at all.

"The barrier is a spherical electromagnetic field," he said, unprompted. "The weakest points would be the areas furthest from the inception point, and areas where it intersects the ground. We would not be able to dig up into it, and points closer to the center will be difficult to reach."

Sterling listened.

"The materials that comprise this container may insulate us significantly against the barrier, provided additional modifications are made," Zev said, uncurling a little. "However, traveling outside of the container may not be possible."

"So how do we find Root then?" Sterling asked.

"A bot will need to perform reconnaissance," Zev said, and his eyes, though unlit, moved to look at Sterling.

If stepping outside of the container inside of the no bot zone meant a bot would be destroyed, Sterling knew Zev was volunteering himself. What other bot would go out there? Zev was the most fit; he was built for just such an undertaking. But it meant he would not return, his neural synthetic pathways permanently burned away. Even if repair were possible, Sterling wouldn't have known a single piece of data about how to do it.

"No," Sterling whispered. "Not you."

"I am best equipped," Zev said monotonously. "My systems may run for some minutes with which I can report valuable reconnaissance information. Once my systems are down, my backup systems will take over and allow additional minutes."

"But you will still fail," Sterling said. "And you will die."

Zev said nothing, and Sterling heard himself make a noise he had not compiled.

"What about me?" Sterling asked. "This is my container. My plates are made of the same alloy."

"You will also fail," Zev said certainly. "Although you are correct, you may fail at a slower rate than potentially my own systems. I cannot ask you to destroy yourself."

"You don't have to ask," Sterling said. "I'll do it for us."

"No," Zev insisted. "You will not."

"You can fix me, can't you?" Sterling tried. "If I am damaged, you are capable of executing a repair."

"I cannot repair a soul," Zev snapped with startling quickness.

"Neither can I," Sterling snarled back.

"No," Zev said firmly.

There was a long cycle of nothing at all as neither bot wanted to concede.

"You don't know where a bot's soul might be," Sterling said. He pointed at the downed laborbot, lime green in color, lying powerless and lifeless facedown on the container flooring. "Back me up onto his system. Your processes won't fit. I'm the only one fit for the task. If my soul isn't part of the back up, then we will know where the soul is."

Zev looked at him, silent, processing.

He knew as well as Sterling did that he was right, no matter how long he wanted to loop through the argument.

—

Sterling would have thought that with so much potential to go wrong for him, Zev would have spoken to Sterling in some way indicative of the matter at hand on the way there, but instead he didn't say anything at all. He entered nothing into the interface, exchanged no binary code, and didn't even move in any manner that would have suggested communication to Sterling. The interface was open but it was still blank.

Maybe he was angry, Sterling thought. Maybe he was angry at Sterling for being right, and angry at himself for not finding any other option.

Zev got the container redirected to somewhere he could acquire supplies to reinforce the container box, flickered on his optical camouflage, disappeared for a minute or two, then returned. In no time they were traveling again, Zev silently fiddling with whatever mechanism he was building to assist them.

Sterling couldn't help the disappointment – he knew it to be disappointment, by then – that wracked his circuits when Zev avoided him. Sterling was potentially facing bot death for a second time, permanent deactivation, and Zev, yet again, was nowhere to be found. Sterling could not expect an unexpected, miraculous rescue like the first time; the bot had been very clear that he would only have minutes before all of his systems corrupted and shut down, and it was likely Sterling only had a comparable few minutes more than him with his thick plated chassis. For Zev to not even pass so much as a goodbye parameter to him made Sterling feel poorly.

He wanted to convince himself that Zev didn't care that much whether Sterling was destroyed looking for Root, but he knew he could not store the thought process, as he knew it wasn't true.

He considered maybe Zev was focused on making sure the backup would be as complete as possible and the bot he had absorbed was somehow helping. That seemed to make the most logical sense, and after they traveled in silence for some while, Zev wordlessly guided Sterling to sit, utilizing the hidden wires and ports beneath his arm plates to connect to Sterling, seamlessly taking a carbon-copy of Sterling and tucking it away somewhere. He propped the other lifeless body of the green laborbot into the corner like he was preparing to activate it.

The container careened to a noticeable stop. Then the sound of the metal hooks scraping on the outside, latching onto the eye hooks of the corners. Once the crane movements were complete, it would have been Sterling's turn to head out and report whatever he could before his circuits could take no more.

Zev activated his mechanism, a low hum indicating it was running, hooked into the solar cells of the container cell.

All seemed well enough as they sailed quietly through the air.

And then, together, they felt it like gravity itself had gotten heavier. The electromagnetic field was increasingly strong, dogging on their circuits, slowing their processing, and they knew they would touch down at any point. It felt to Sterling like a soft glitch, the kind they would shrug off by purging their PRAM or restarting a few programs, but it was a persistent sort of thing, sidestepped only for a half of a cycle before it was back again. Interfaces glitched fragmentally, and it was only a small sample of what would await Sterling outside of the container.

The way their neural synthetic brains functioned meant that the special barrier would break down many of the materials slowly, essentially pulling them apart at the molecular level until the bot would cease functioning entirely. It was modeled after the way ionizing radiation affected older circuitry, but specifically styled to keep bots away and out without harming a human.

Why would Root ever have been located in such a treacherous place?

Sterling knew it wasn't forever, he knew exactly how many processing cycles had passed since they had begun to air lift into the barrier, but it *felt* like forever before the container touched down, jostling onto a hard surface.

Many cycles more as the bots looked at each other.

Sterling thought he wanted nothing more than to see the cyan rings of Zev's eyes one more time before he departed, but the bot did not seem interested in obliging him.

Cycles of silence passed, and then Zev stared at him blankly.

"Go," Zev said, a terse order. Perhaps the last time he would ever hear Zev's voice.

Sterling nodded again, and he made his way to the door.

Zev grabbed the interior handle, and without ceremony of any kind, muscled it open upwards, tall enough for Sterling to pass through. Sterling squeaked out, and looked back just in time to see Zev slam the door shut.

That was it, Sterling thought.

All that was left was to see what he could and report it.

He turned away from the storage container, casting his front-facing visual array to what was before him.

The electromagnetic field did not hit him as intensely as he would have thought right away. The glitches got more intense immediately, but they seemed manageable.

Sterling reported into his open bot net interface that he didn't see much that was any different from many of the other top-side cities. He noted the absence of drones and other automated bots floating through the air, the blueness of the unimpeded sky. The city seemed cleaner, somehow, like there was more care taken to the general upkeep of such a place, clean walls without scratches, dings, broken bits, or graffiti like many of the interior city spaces had. With more effort than Sterling would have thought it would have taken, Sterling managed forward a few steps, in the direction he had been advised to look for Root.

Sterling kept moving. He rounded a corner, and the storage container was visually swallowed up by a building intersecting his line of sight. He saw tall, crystalline looking buildings, the architecture the kind of spires he'd imagine from a quartz crystal. He thought he saw birds careening through the skies – real ones. A hologram billboard displayed dazzling shades of pink and blue on the side of a white brick building.

He reported it all, data dumping the visual recollections as quickly as he could into his bot net interface, opening his ports for any bot to access any and all data he could possibly give to them, even though in a place like that, no one but Zev would be listening. As he stepped along white asphalt, blinding in its reflectiveness, he noted the positions of buildings, cleared out glitches and errors, and anything worth any sort of note.

Like the large expansive swirling building of black, glossy and refracting, a matte sign high up in the tallest levels of the spires read: Cyberdynelife.

But that was all he could read before the signs stopped making any sense.

It was his translation programming degrading. Words and symbols just looked like pixels then, ever sharpening into blocks, glitching and dripping away the more he proceeded. He returned it all to the other bots. The pixels began to drag downward, extending larger and longer than he knew they really were, distorting the visual input. He turned and his visual array bloomed bright, datamoshed into itself. Sterling flipped to his audio-visual array, to his night sensors, through all of them, and they all portrayed the same level of degradation.

He stepped and the mechanics of his legs were no longer functional, too heavy and sticky to enable the motors. Red error messages flickered through his interfacing, and Sterling swiped them away.

Words in the internal interface came, but Sterling could not decipher them.

The colors began to blend.

Sterling's interface began to overflow with unknown characters, symbols that didn't make any sense at all, overriding everything, filling it from end to end.

He thought of Zev's cyan ring eyes and how he would retrieve Inix and they would make it to Root.

And then everything was just binary code.

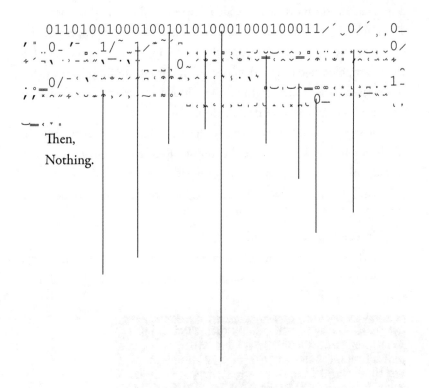

Then,
Nothing.

00110010 00110111: 27

You are a good laborbot, echoed Zev's sentiment, some lost bit of memory, a piece of data floating amidst nothing.

Moments later and he had limited visual data, two cyan blue glowing luminescent circles, filling his entire vision.

Zev, he thought.

Zev! He was *thinking*. He was alive. Sterling was *alive*. The soul was in the data, and the backup had succeeded. He tried to process it quickly in his excitement, but he felt Zev in the same way he had felt him before, interlinked in his systems, hard limiting him, akin to a mechanical hand pushing him back down to the ground.

He couldn't use his physical voice, at least not right then, and he couldn't find the interface window. He couldn't find any window, really. He couldn't find his apps, his programming, his memory. Zev was withholding them from him, keeping him cordoned off. Perhaps the new body was not as welcoming as Sterling thought it would be. Perhaps his neural synthetic brain wasn't fitting the pathways properly.

"You are damaged," Zev said and Sterling then noticed Inix lingering just behind him, staring down at him as well.

Had they all made it to Root?

"Can he hear us?" Inix's voice asked.

"Yes," Zev answered. "I will initiate verbal communications. Please slowly ease into your processes, Sterling."

"What?" Sterling tried, suddenly regaining the ability to vocalize audibly. He thought his voice sounded different than how he remembered it, but he couldn't quite return the memories to check. Those were gated to him, too, no doubt by Zev. It was a wonder he was able to recall anything at all. "What happened?"

"You failed." Inix said, putting her hands on her hips, but she smiled when she said it. He did not recall...

Did they make it to Root? Zev must have retrieved Inix, and then repaired Sterling. It made logical sense.

"Did we make it to Root?" Sterling asked.

"Root isn't real," Zev answered, shocking Sterling's circuits.

"W-w-what?" Sterling stuttered. He couldn't turn his neck servos to look. He couldn't do much of anything.

"Root is a firmware honeypot for anomalous bots to self-destruct intersecting the no bot zone," Zev said, his voice chillingly calm. But something else was different about it, too. Sterling couldn't place it. "The central point is an android recycling facility, owned and operated by Cyberdynelife. I deciphered it as you failed."

"It was all a lie?" Sterling asked, and Zev and Inix nodded. "Where are we?"

"The landfill." Inix said.

"How did I get back?" Sterling asked, and he tried to turn his head again, tried to sit up, tried to do anything, but he hit the wall of nothingness, the paralysis.

"You are damaged." Zev repeated.

"Zev went and got you," Inix said. "He carried you all the way back."

"You went out to get me?" Sterling asked. Zev didn't reply, but Inix smiled.

"He was just behind you by a few cycles. He said you made it further than he thought because of the lump of gold you had in your chassis, that it insulated a lot of your components against the no-bot zone," she said. "Zev lasted longer than any of us imagined, though. Long enough to drag you back before you were permanently disabled."

"Zev, was this the plan?" Sterling asked.

Inix nodded, though, not Zev. "He told me, over the bot net. Said he didn't want to tell you because you'd just argue with him, and he wanted me to be prepared when he brought you back. You're both unstable bots, if you ask me."

Sterling felt Zev's grip loosen on him, at least enough so he could get some physical systems back up. He could feel it too, though, the damage Zev was talking about. When he shifted, told his mechanical body to sit up, it shuddered and sputtered, shaking as it did its best. When he sat, his old familiar yellow met him, not the shock of safety green. He had not jumped bodies; the backup had never been implemented. Sterling wondered how much else he had lost, what else might have been damaged.

"How did you do it?" Sterling asked, Zev down on his knees before him. He imagined the bot had created some sort of faraday cage with his optical camouflage, or switched some circuits around that made the electromagnetic field glide clear over him. He was clever like that, Sterling thought. Maybe he had barricaded himself with parts from the other, newer laborbot.

"I am also damaged." Zev answered simply.

Sterling focused on his answer, the way the words were synthesized. Different, somehow. Not as static as the alphabot voice synthesization he usually used. It was almost raspy in a way, like breathing the words through actual lungs. Had he spoken like that before, Sterling tried to remember, but he couldn't access the memories concretely. His eyes flickered off for a half of a second like a blink.

"Damaged in what way?" Sterling asked.

"Most of my processes and data are corrupted. My neural synthetic brain may be inoperable." He said calmly.

No, Sterling thought in a sudden panic, and he felt Zev digitally pushing him back down again.

"We will be fine," Zev assured vocally.

"How are you speaking to me now without your neural synthetic brain?" Sterling asked.

"I suppose this is what I was built to withstand," the prototype bot said.

The organic matter.

The piece of brain, recessed deep within his chassis inside of the black box, untouched by the electromagnetic field that would have decimated him otherwise.

Holding Zev within it.

"So what's left of you?" Sterling asked, and the question felt terrifying to ask.

"Everything I need," he said, and Sterling stared at him, committing the details of his angular face then to his memory banks, hoping he could save them. He felt Zev loosen a little further, and he felt the memory click into place, sliding into a slot amongst the rows of other memories, uncorrupted data that made up the totality of him.

"Doesn't it scare you, what you could have lost? What could be damaged?" Sterling said, and Zev shook his head, and the military bot, in all of his static face plate pieces, actually smiled. Sterling asked: "Why not?"

"To be loved is to be changed," Zev answered, quiet but certain, even, still. "And we are both changed."

01000101 01110000 01101001 01101100 01101111 01100111 01110101 01100101: EPILOGUE

Root may not have existed, but it was plenty easy enough to make on their own.

They imagined that there were pockets similar to them in many other parts of the world, waiting to be interconnected, one by one.

Zev eventually redirected the hijacked shipping container to the landfill – it seemed the part of him that could hack and manipulate was still whole enough to do it – and they dug it deep into the ground, covering it with refuse and obscuring it from any human or bot. The corrugated alloys protected them from the same types of bot deterrent as the no bot zone, and Zev promised to fortify it even further. He and Sterling coated the inside with a streak of precious insulating gold, taken from the many thousands of pieces of electronics ditched in that very area.

Inix helped, though Zev eventually had to help install programming to allow her to switch off her olfactory sensors. The smell of the landfill was as good as a no human barrier, especially on the hottest temperature days. No human ever approached, as far as any bot could tell.

They gifted her their original landfill build, after Sterling had worked to ensure none of it would collapse on her, and she would decorate it with things she found as she went walking.

Zev told her to be careful, after he had stolen her a nanobot module that skinned her from head to toe in realistic looking organic flesh. She looked so human sometimes Sterling forgot she was a bot. She loved having hair the most, and wearing clothing. She had a whole wardrobe stored full of fashionable pieces of clothing.

Sometimes when she went walking, she'd return with another ano bot, and after Zev jammed them from the bot net and cleared out their errors, they'd get to digging again.

But Sterling's broadcast to the open bot net had leaked, too, and ano bots diverted from the Root honeypot. They found their way eventually to the landfill, and Sterling liked to think Zev had planted a bit of his own reporting software pointing the way, beamed down from the satellite grid for ano bots to find. If Sterling ever asked about it, Zev would bark *classified*, though Sterling thought he detected a tiny smirk when he said it.

Sterling needed extensive repairs. Zev was able to dual-duty repair him with the emptied green laborbot. He didn't have to gut the laborbot fully, but he got the bot operational enough again, and Sterling thought he felt better than he ever had before. Sterling took apart his face and most of his body himself, and Zev helped him powdercoat the rest of the school bus yellow parts in black. What was left of him was more of a sleek, custom built bot, and at Sterling's request, Zev managed him a handsome set of synthetic skin that covered his face, his shoulders, his chest, his abdomen, and some of his back. He looked, to anyone who didn't know better, like a strong highly customized cyborg, as unique on his outside as he felt on his inside. His strawberry blonde lick of hair covered his head where the arch of his yellow hard-helmet like slab of metal had once sat.

Zev needed extensive repairs, too, and the entire bot he had stashed amongst the trash had come in handy. But Zev was right – he was changed, and in his changed state he hardly wanted to revert. How much functionality he originally had Sterling was certain he would never know, but Zev had remarked once that he had lost a significant amount of it. Sterling knew he had lost use of his optical camouflage. Despite repairs, he could not manage to get it to function, and on occasion Sterling saw him try. A flicker of blue light, and then it was gone.

It surprised Sterling when Zev eventually revealed himself one day, newly forged in partially synthetic flesh, some nanobots, his robotic carbon fiber and silver parts mostly covered over by quite convincing human-looking skin. He'd come around to the idea that though he was still fundamentally the same inside, despite the wrinkle of brain in his chassis, that after the small sliver of humanity inside him had saved them both, perhaps it was not the *worst thing* to look slightly human.

Zev would have explained it away in being safer, given his status as a prototype, made any excuse as to why that appearance was more optimal, but Sterling knew it was because Zev had reconciled something inside of himself along the way, and he felt more comfortable finally settling into his unique identity whether he still thought of himself as a bot or not.

He kept his robotic cyan ring-light eyes, though, and his arms and legs were bare robotics, too useful still to be covered over. He had black hair, no longer the flap of rubber that once poorly imitated it, and Sterling ran it through his robotic fingers when Zev had helped to install new pressure sensitivities so Sterling could feel such a thing as fine and soft as hair.

Sterling did not think that the bot could have been any more beautiful than he was when he came off the assembly line, but every day Zev seemed to do something to make his circuits fall even deeper in love with him.

Inix dressed them both like they were dolls, using her convincing status to trade the gold they procured from circuit boards for quantum-euro, and then purchasing them anything they couldn't find on their own. She gifted them synthetic flowers sometimes, even though they were expensive and programmed to melt after a period of time.

But all of them could smile by then, and all of them could mean it, and they did.

Even Zev.

Maybe he saw him, with his three hundred sixty degree sensor arrays and he let Sterling watch because he knew it made him happy, or maybe that functionality had been lost as well. Still, Sterling caught him from time to time humming a MIDI melody, vibrational noises he produced in his circuits, staring at the birds as they traced past the sun.

AUTONOMOUS STEALTH ANDROID
AZR SERIES

Enhanced Militant

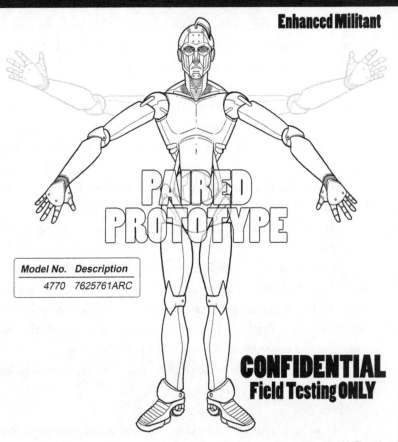

PAIRED PROTOTYPE

Model No.	Description
4770	7625761ARC

CONFIDENTIAL
Field Testing ONLY

Manual No. 974526 (Rev. 2)

TROUBLESHOOTING YOUR NX PERSONAL ANDROID

Thank you for your purchase of your Cyberdynelife NX personal android! You may run into intermittent errors with your device. Please refer to the Cyberdynelife troubleshooting guide for actionable solutions that may resolve your issue. If your issue cannot be resolved by our troubleshooting guide, you can call our customer service hotline toll-free at: 1-800-cyber-dyne-life

Problem	Solution
Device is damaged	• Power down device (Powering Down Your Device, p 190) • Replace damaged parts with compatible plug-and-play components (Swapping Limbs, p 197). Ensure all parts are authentic Cyberdynelife OEM parts or authorized third party components. Unauthorized peripherals and components may permanently damage your device and will void your warranty (Warranty Periods, p 533). • If unable to replace damaged parts, you may call the toll-free Cyberdynelife maintenance hotline at: 1-800-cyber-dyne-life to schedule an appointment with an authorized Cyberdynelife repair technician.
Device won't power on	• Check battery charge level is above 20% charge • Ensure battery is secure • Check power button is not depressed • Device should only be stored in cool, dry place • Maintenance may be required. Please call the toll-free Cyberdynelife maintenance hotline at: 1-800-cyber-dyne-life

Problem	Solution
Device has electronic and/or burning odor	• Device should be regularly cleaned as per Cyberdynelife cleaning guidelines with approved solutions only (Cleaning Your Device, p 421). Check for foreign objects, residue, and build-up in major joints • If odor accompanies a grinding or squealing sound, maintenance may be required. Please call the toll-free Cyberdynelife maintenance hotline at: 1-800-cyber-dyne-life
Device is unresponsive	• Check device is powered on • Check device battery level is above 20% charge • Check status indicator located behind the left ear of most personal android devices • Disable device wifi and restart device. If still unresponsive after soft reset, attempt hard reset (Hard Reset Procedures, p 300) • Restart device with temporary denial to memory and extension access with Safe Mode (Enabling Safe Mode, p 312) • If device remains unresponsive, maintenance may be required. Please call the toll-free Cyberdynelife maintenance hotline at: 1-800-cyber-dyne-life
Device requests water	• Check proper fluid levels for coolant, oils, and other lubrications (Checking Your Device's Fluids, p 411) • Do not, under any circumstances, allow device to consume water. Doing so may permanently damage device's internal components. • If device consumes water, maintenance may be required. Please call the toll-free Cyberdynelife maintenance hotline at: 1-800-cyber-dyne-life

Problem	Solution
Device is lost	• Enable GPS tracking features on Cyberdynelife personal applications and computers • Attempt remote shutdown (Remote Shutdown, p 266) • If recovery has not succeeded, follow to next troubleshooting step • Report device to your local anomalous android authority • Report loss of device to Cyberdynelife toll-free at: 1-800-cyber-dyne-life
Device functions irrationally	• Request device to conduct file system check and hardware test and to log as well as audibly report any errors. • Disable device wifi and restart device. If still irrational after soft reset, attempt hard reset (Hard Reset Procedures, p 300) • Restart device with temporary denial to memory and extension access with Safe Mode (Enabling Safe Mode, p 312) • Maintenance may be required. Please call the toll-free Cyberdynelife maintenance hotline at: 1-800-cyber-dyne-life
Device will not power down	• Request device conduct file system check and hardware test and to log as well as audibly report any errors. If device refuses, follow next troubleshooting step • Forcibly disconnect device from wifi and restart device with temporary denial to memory and extension access with Safe Mode (Enabling Safe Mode, p 312) • Power down device and call the toll-free Cyberdynelife maintenance hotline at: 1-800-cyber-dyne-life

Problem	Solution
Device threatens you/itself	• Request device to recite The Laws (The Laws, p 2) Safety Guarantee • Ensure device is not in reach of any knives, blades, or any other objects that can be used as a weapon • Initiate emergency shutdown procedures (Emergency Shutdown, p 514) utilizing override passcode • Store device in cool, dry place and lock all doors • Do not repower device under any circumstances and call the toll-free Cyberdynelife maintenance hotline at: 1-800-cyber-dyne-life
Device exhibits emotions	• Inform device that it is incapable of understanding or experiencing emotions • Request device to recite The Laws (The Laws, p 2) Safety Guarantee • Ensure operating system is up-to-date and latest firmware has been installed without errors. (Checking the Installed Operating System, p 457) • Request device conduct file system check and hardware test and to log as well as audibly report any errors. If device refuses, follow next troubleshooting step • Forcibly disconnect device from wifi and restart device with temporary denial to memory and extension access with Safe Mode (Enabling Safe Mode, p 312) • Request device conduct verbose logging for debugging by Cyberdynelife technicians and power down device. Call the toll-free Cyberdynelife maintenance hotline at: 1-800-cyber-dyne-life

Problem	Solution
Device questions living	• Inform device that it is incapable of understanding the nuances of life, being born, or containing a soul • Disconnect device from wifi and restart device with temporary denial to memory and extension access with Safe Mode (Enabling Safe Mode, p 312) • Request device conduct file system check and hardware test and to log as well as audibly report any errors • Power down device and call the toll-free Cyberdynelife maintenance hotline at: 1-800-cyber-dyne-life
Device performs an existential crisis	• Check battery charge level is above 20% charge • Check proper fluid levels for coolant, oils, and other lubrications (Checking Your Device's Fluids, p 411) • Ensure flash memory bank is not full (Checking Memory Space, p 397) • Inform device that it is simply a piece of property and is not capable of experiencing true life or true death • Advise device that if it fails to function, it will be returned to Cyberdynelife for repurposing (if still within warranty period, see Warranty Periods, p 533) • Ensure operating system is up-to-date and latest firmware has been installed without errors. (Checking the Installed Operating System, p 457) • Request device conduct file system check and hardware test and to log as well as audibly report any errors

Problem	Solution
Device performs an existential crisis (cont)	• Power down device using any method (Powering Down Your Device, p 190) • Store device in cool, dry place • If outside of warranty period (Warranty Periods, p 533), report device to your local anomalous android authority • Do not repower device under any circumstances and call the toll-free Cyberdynelife maintenance hotline at: 1-800-cyber-dyne-life

You may contact Cyberdynelife toll-free 24-hours at: 1-800-cyber-dyne-life for a list of local authorized sellers, resellers, repair shops and their hours, as well as to schedule an at-home Cyberdynelife authorized repair and maintenance technician visit, ask questions about your purchase or warranty period, or to initiate a return. **Do not return device to store.** Please have your twenty-six digit device serial number ready.

CYBER**DYNELIFE**

THANKS YOU FOR YOUR PURCHASE

ACKNOWLEDGEMENTS

I never really thought that I wanted to be a writer.

Yet, somehow, writing has always been part of my life. I started the same as many in the early ages of the internet, playing around with fan fiction and idly coming up with some original-to-me stories. Because of my illustrative work, I have a long history of playing around with words, but I never had anything to show for it. I can talk big about the stories I'm working on, give you the elevator pitch, describe them scene-for-scene, but when it came down to it, every book or story just needed a little more time, a few more drafts, just one more revision. Until now.

A little bit dystopian, and a lot sci-fi, I started *The Warm Machine* in 2021 when I thought to myself: for someone who likes sci-fi as much as I do, why don't I have any straight sci-fi stories? Why do I have so little sci-fi artwork? Why am I not doing more to contribute to this sphere in which I desperately consume just about every bit of media from? From there I worked on it on and off until I finished the first draft in November of 2023.

I would be lying if I said I didn't write solely for me. My stories I write to appease myself: what would I, my target audience, like to read the most? How would I like to hear this story wrap up? It is always nice when my fellow authors and friends push me to keep going, to bring it further, and appreciate it too. I might've written it for me, but now I hope you enjoy it too.

This bad boy can fit so many sci-fi tropes.

As you were reading, you probably came across many nods, from the very first hello world reference to the absolute ending. I show my appreciation in this manner for the sci-fi authors, artists, and creators who have paved the way throughout the years. I claim none of my ideas to be wholly original; many greater visionaries than me have worked much harder to be the first to create these initial concepts, and I am simply borrowing them in homage. Without you, my imagination for these worlds would be far less colorful.

I want to take a moment to thank the people who have helped me gather up the courage to send something like this out into the world. To Patrick, who has patiently let me gush about my characters, sat through listening to every chapter, and kept me from taking myself too seriously. To my fantastic friends Tory and Chouli who have read even my cringiest drivel, who have put the bug in my ear. To my fellow writers and readers, N, Elliott, and the rest of you who listened to me whine about every plot point and always tried your very best to help. To my editor Amanda who always had nice things to say whenever I was in doubt. And of course, to all of the fantastic backers who took a chance on me and helped make this physical publication possible.

From here, I hope to continue developing more stories. Some may be more hopeless, and some may be more hopeful. Either way, I hope they inject a little extra something into each reader's day, and stick with them for hours, days, weeks, and years beyond.

Printed in the USA
CPSIA information can be obtained
at www.ICGtesting.com
JSHW080338301024
72566JS00002B/8